Santa Sarah Genesis

How the Kringle's became
Mr. and Mrs. Santa Claus

By

Ron Krzyzan

ACKNOWLEDGMENTS

I would like to acknowledge four wonderful women.

Pat Lindholm, for her advice and encouragement that gave me the motivation to continue when I had my doubts.

Mary Kathleen Dougherty, who led me through the process.

My daughter Kim Yantz, whose suggestions were greatly appreciated.

My wife Jo, who was always there.

To PT

Merry Christmas

Ron

DEDICATION

To Meghan, who left us too soon.

CHAPTER 1

David Carson was either unconscious or in a deep sleep. It didn't really matter, he was totally unaware of his surroundings. Gradually his body and then his mind began to stir. His right arm twitched. His eyebrows moved up and down as if that would help him open his eyes. He unclenched his fist and turned his palm upward, facing the ceiling. David moved his head slowly side to side as if he was trying to say no.

There are many ways to come out of a deep sleep. Some people wake quickly while others take awhile. Unfortunately, David was awaking very slowly. In his line of work, this was not a good thing.

Bit by bit his mind and body were becoming aware of the situation. Through this murky haze, his training told him that caution was needed. He heard sounds and thought, "Could this be a hospital?"

There was an antiseptic smell, something he couldn't quite identify. "I don't think I'm dead." He lay there with his eyes closed for what seemed like a long time. He was unsure if he wanted to see where he was. At least he wasn't freezing; the air on his face was pleasantly warm. He wasn't lying on a cold block of ice.

David was one of two agents that were sent to the Arctic to evaluate what an American satellite detected.

A polar orbiting satellite detected and photographed what appeared to be buildings near the North Pole area of the Arctic.

American surveillance planes were sent to the North Pole region to verify that data. Three surveillance flights on three different days did not confirm what the satellite detected. Yet the satellite on those three days still showed construction in the area. On the fourth day, the satellite showed no buildings or construction. Only ice and snow.

This raised some red flags in the US Defense Department. One theory suggested that a foreign country, most likely the Soviet Union, had developed a new type of camouflage. When their radar detected an airplane, the camouflage would be activated. The thought was that the radar could detect airplanes but was unable to detect a satellite. In that situation, the camouflage was not deployed. It was assumed that those controlling the concealment equipment realized this weakness and made adjustments to keep their base hidden.

A Soviet base at the North Pole would pose a dangerous situation for the security of United States. Both the United States and the Soviet Union had large stockpiles of Intercontinental Ballistic Nuclear Missiles. Firing those missiles from such a close range would be a huge advantage. United States missile launching bases would be defenseless and would be destroyed before the United States could retaliate.

After all, it is 1961, and the United States and the Soviet Union are involved in a nuclear arms race. Tensions are very high. Both sides feared that the enemy might launch an early preemptive strike with nuclear weapons. There would be a war, but it would be over in a few short hours. The losing side would be completely annihilated.

The Berlin Wall was erected in August of 1961. At the end of October, the United States and the Soviet Union tanks faced each other no more than 100 yards apart, separated only by the Wall. The slightest incident could have caused a hair trigger response. The Cold War was in full bloom.

Many ideas were considered to determine the most feasible way of investigating what was really happening at the North Pole. Was there actually a military base there? Were they friends or foes? There was no doubt, the US had to find out who or what was there.

The options ranged from dangerous to cautious. Dangerous in that it could get out of hand. Tensions were so high that it could possibly lead to a war. At the other extreme, the most cautious scenario was to do nothing.

The only option was very involved and extremely dangerous. The US Air Force Base in Thule, Greenland would be the operational headquarters. It is, about 750 miles from the North Pole. That distance eliminated many of the possible tactics. Snowmobiles were considered but ruled out because of noise, distance, and reliability at those extreme temperatures.

The plan was to use dogsled teams to covertly approach the suspected area. Cargo planes would parachute the dog sleds and equipment to a specified location.

The nuclear submarine USS Skate 578 would transport two CIA agents and their sled dogs to within 30 miles from the target location by surfacing through the ice. At the completion of the mission, the agents and the dogs would use the Skate to return home.

As David was slowly becoming more alert, it struck him... "I am alive... alive in a hospital!" He carefully tried to open his eyes, hoping not to be discovered as being awake. He needed more time, more clues, anything that would help him understand the situation he was in. He didn't know if he was rescued or captured.

When he finally opened his eyes, David expected to see a hospital room. He realized that his bed was made up of two smaller beds that were pushed together. He wondered if this was a children's hospital or possibly a school of some sort.

His mind went back to the mission. He'd survived the earthquake. Someone was able to save him. The last thing David remembered was trying to save himself and the dogs from getting dragged into the icy water by the sled. It had quickly tipped to one side, part of it falling into the water where solid ice had been an instant before. "Oh my God," he yelled, "I'm going to lose the sled."

Another sound quickly regained his attention. He was now fully awake, exiting the haze that he was in a few seconds ago. "I need to stay focused, this is not the time to panic," David thought.

He knew he could not have gotten there by himself. His ankle was injured and it would be impossible for him to cross the icy open water. Someone had to have brought him here. He wondered if his dogs survived. They were the reason that he even made it this far. What about the other team? Are they safe? Were they able to accomplish the mission?

David never thought that this mission was really necessary. Risking the lives of two agents and their dog teams in the dead of winter was dangerous and possibly even suicidal.

The smells and sounds convinced him that he was in a hospital. The first order of business was that he must learn with whom he was dealing with. If he was in enemy hands, they might try to trick him into thinking he was safe. The enemy might want to gain his trust to obtain information from him about why he was here and what he was doing. If he was in friendly hands, they might not be aware of the mission due to the secrecy of it. What if the other team was in trouble too? They also might need rescuing. It was a dilemma, it was a secret mission, and he had to keep it that way. He had to be sure not to divulge anything about the mission.

David's mind went back to the incident; the last thing he remembered was that he was probably going to freeze to death. When he cut the lines, he also sliced through the fabric of his coveralls. There was a sharp jolt as icy salt water filled his boot and pant leg up to his knee. There was no possibility to remove his boot and to dry his foot. All the equipment he could use went down with the sled when he cut the lines to save the dogs.

More sounds, murmuring, voices, higher pitched than you would expect in a hospital. Could they be children? He thought about getting out of bed to investigate but he needed more information. He decided to lie still and let them come to him. "You make the first move," he whispered to himself.

His mind flashed back to the other agent and his dogs. They only knew each other by their code names. That was by design to protect the families of the agents. Each member of the team had a specialty. Big burly Richard, a mountain of a man was an expert in celestial navigation. David's expertise was in the Russian language. He was also the most experienced in this frigid environment they encountered because he was born and raised in Alaska.

When World War II broke out, David, like millions of other young Americans, joined the Army. He saw action in the Aleutian Islands, a chain of almost deserted volcanic islands that jut out from the mainland of Alaska. His unit managed to repel the Japanese from the area.

David remained in the Army and eventually became one of the elite Army Rangers. He became an officer in command of a unit that specialized in fighting in cold weather climates. His training became very valuable because within five years of the end of World War II, the Korean War broke out.

He saw action for several months but unfortunately was captured and became a prisoner of war. His prison cell was located where he could hear his captors. Some of those conversations were in Russian, a language in which David was fluent. David overheard a conversation that brainwashing was being planned by his captors. He was able to assist his fellow prisoners into understanding what the enemy was trying to do.

After the war he was recruited by the Central Intelligence Agency as a Russian language interpreter. The CIA quickly realized that he had more specialized skills and trained him in intelligence–gathering and other covert fields.

Living in a remote area of Alaska, he learned to drive a dog sled at a very early age. His language skills, his cold weather training, his intelligence gathering skills, and being able to drive a dog sled made him perfect for this operation.

When the United States purchased Alaska from Russia in 1867, Russian citizens became American citizens overnight. The language and customs remained Russian for many years. David's parents worked, so his grandmother helped to raise him. She taught him to speak Russian, and he became fluent in both English and Russian.

David's wife, Liz was not happy about him having to leave on what looked like a dangerous mission just before Christmas. "Haven't you given them enough?" she said. "Can't it wait for just a few days until after Christmas?" she continued.

"It has to be very important, or they wouldn't ask me to do this." said David.

"Will you be home by Christmas?"

"I certainly hope so," he said not very convincingly.

David knew a mission like this was not something that could be finished in a few days.

The two men were highly trained, disciplined, and physically and mentally strong. Yet this mission worried them. They met privately to discuss the risks and rewards of this operation. They did agree reluctantly, because their patriotism and love of country won out. They gave the okay and the mission would start in four days. David wrote a "Good Bye" letter to his wife and two daughters, hoping that it would never have to be delivered. Both men spent a restless night and yet when the time came, it was a go.

The nuclear sub Skate was designed to use space efficiently. Adding two men and 16 dogs made the ship impossibly crowded. The crew enjoyed having the dogs on board but after three days at sea, the strain on everyone was evident.

David and Richard marveled at the idea that a sub could surface through the ice of the Arctic. The captain assured them, "I was a little nervous the first time we did it. It's going to make a lot of noise, but they built the ship the right way. We'll be fine."

It did make a lot of noise. The crunching of the ice against the hull reminded Richard of some recent unpleasant dental work. The two agents were happy when the captain gave the crew orders to open the hatch. A few minutes later he gave the guests permission to leave the ship. David climbed the ladder and walked out onto the deck. The extreme cold was expected, but it shocked him.

"Brace yourself Richard, it's cold out here."

"Really?" said Richard in a mocking sarcastic tone.

The Arctic is dark for 24 hours at this time of the year. The only light came from a blaze of stars and the Aurora Borealis. Richard easily located the black colored parachutes lying on the white background of snow. The sleds were approximately three hundred yards away. Richard went about cutting the sleds and equipment free from the parachutes. The drop went extremely well. Two planes were used so that the drop would fall in a confined space. They found that the equipment was in excellent condition.

David, with the help of three crewmen, got the dogs out of the sub. One of the crew members would hoist the dog up and another would lead the dog to David who would attach it to the harness. The third crew member controlled the dogs who were already in the harness.

It took but a few minutes to complete the harnessing. The two agents exchanged handshakes and salutes with the captain and crew members. They quickly began mushing their way to the objective. The Skate slowly began to recede back into the ocean to wait for them to return.

The dogs were trained to keep their barking to a minimum while pulling the sled. For the most part they did. They had to travel approximately 25 miles over the sometimes rough Arctic ice pack. It was a dangerous crossing for the dogs. If they failed, the men were very much in jeopardy.

The sky was clear. The stars were flickering brilliant points of light, creating enough light for them to easily keep track of each other. The very cold snow made a crunching sound as the runners furrowed their way toward their destination. It was the same sound that he remembered making as a youngster when walking to church late at night on Christmas Eve. David thought, "Returning home for Christmas might not happen this year."

The plan was for David's team to take the lead with Richard's team trailing and off to the port side. They would communicate with hand signals. Radio silence was in effect and would not be used unless there was an extreme emergency. The Arctic ice pack surface was relatively smooth but did have outcrops. Storms created waves that disrupted the ice surface, leaving scattered ice monuments.

Then, unexpectedly, it happened. There was a loud crack and a violent eruption of icy salt water as it shot into the air. The sled and runner on the right side was no longer on ice, but rather submerged in the icy water. The sled seemed to come alive, almost as if it was a rodeo bull trying to shake a rider off. The sled turned on its side and was starting to slip off the ice, almost causing David to follow it into the now open water. The wheel dogs, Bonnie and Clyde, were in the water and were in danger of being pulled down by the sinking sled. David was awkwardly trying to maintain his balance as the sled tipped even more. The dogs ahead of Bonnie and Clyde were dry, but were straining and clawing to regain their footing on the slippery ice.

He had to make a decision, he could save himself or try to save the sled and the dogs. More of the sled slid off the solid ice, so that half of it was underwater. It was tilted to the right side. David leaned to the opposite direction in an effort to straighten it. He knew it would stay buoyant for a short time.

Then the sled completely rolled onto its side and David slipped into the water. It now appeared that there was no hope of saving the sled or any of the provisions. It was going to sink, and sink quickly. His coveralls were waterproof and somewhat buoyant. He paddled his way to where the dogs were still on the ice and pulled himself up and out of the water.

He was in a no-win situation. The sled was sinking and the dogs were soon to follow. Saving the dogs became a priority. He began cutting the lines. He had a better chance of survival if he had the dogs with him. The dogs could be used to keep him warm for a period of time, there was no way to save the sled. His favorite pair, Bonnie and Clyde, were struggling to keep their heads out of the water. It appeared that there was little chance that he could save these two.

Suddenly a wave shoved a slab of ice under the back of the sled and pushed it up and out of the water. David quickly moved towards the sled, hoping this was a stroke of good luck and he would be able to save the sled. Bonnie and Clyde were also pushed onto another small island of ice. Another wave caused the sled to slip back into the water. Instinctively David jumped the short gap of icy ocean water to the island where the dogs were. He began cutting the thick straps that separated the sled from the dogs. He was slicing feverishly through the last strap when the sled pulled him and the dog team back into the water.

There was a terrifying tug on his leg. A strap was tangled between his knee and foot. It twisted and turned his ankle into an unnatural position. The sled was on one side of a block of ice and he was on the other. The dogs were now free of the sled, but he wasn't.

David struggled to untangle himself from the strap that was still attached to the sled. It was difficult to reach his ankle because of his bulky suit. The strap was pulling him closer and closer to the ice block. Finally, his leg crashed into the ice block, pinning him. He only had a few seconds before the strap would slip off the ice block and he would be pulled under... He feverishly slashed at the thick leather strap and finally, he was free.

He knew that he not only cut the strap, but he also cut his pant leg and his ankle might be broken. His boot and pant leg filled with ice water. He didn't have much time, water at that temperature causes hypothermia that saps your body heat and causes your muscles to lose the ability to do their job.

Bonnie and Clyde were at the edge of the ice shelf, struggling to get out of the water. David swam towards them as quickly as he could in his bulky coveralls. He reached the edge of the ice where the dogs were and pushed first Bonnie, then Clyde, to safety. All the dogs were now out of the water. They were free and took off running, dragging the final two along with them. David reached up to save himself but was only able to get one arm and his good leg onto the ice. His water–logged leg was too heavy to lift out of the water. How ironic, that here in the middle of the Cold War, it would be the cold that would do him in.

He heard a familiar sound. The team was back! No barking, just a little squeak, a sound that anyone who had a big dog would recognize. It was his lead dog,

Rex. He took David's pant leg with his teeth and pulled. Two more tugs and David was out.

It took a few minutes for David to regain his breath. The ice surface and splashing water had calmed down. He stood up to test his ankle. It was painful but hopefully not broken.

He looked and listened for any evidence of the other team. No sounds, and they were nowhere to be seen. Things were looking bleak. A sore leg and he was getting colder by the second. Could it get any worse?

David knew that the dogs were acclimated to this cold weather. But even they could not last very long under these conditions. The dogs could keep him warm for a period of time, until they too would not be able to survive.

The wind seemed to be steering his small island of ice, moving it further away from the direction he just came from. His survival training kicked in. He couldn't walk very far, but he knew that he had to find shelter. Someone would have to come to save him.

"We're still alive guys," he said to his dogs. They looked at him and cocked their heads to one side as dogs often do as if to say, "What do we need to do?" Luckily, David found a snow drift nearby that would suit his purpose. He began digging an entrance for a snow cave. It took about twenty minutes to excavate enough snow to make the cave large enough for the dogs and himself.

David unhitched the dogs from the harness, crawled into the cave, and called the dogs to join him. The swirling snow began to accumulate, partially covering the caves' opening, effectively blocking out the wind.

Although the temperature outside was far below zero, it was relatively comfortable in the cave. It was dark, but having his team with him gave him solace. David was exhausted. He put his hands to his face, lowered his head to his chest, closed his eyes and fell asleep.

David woke up with a start. The cave was dark but he realized that this was not a bad dream. The warmth of the dogs kept him somewhat comfortable. The dogs were not only a mode of transportation and the source of warmth, they were his companions. These dogs need thousands of calories each day, but now with the sled gone, they had no food. "Do I sacrifice one or two of them for the good of the team?" he thought. He was starting to think of the unthinkable, there must be another way.

"This is no time to start feeling sorry for ourselves," he said to his companions. "We need to get up and see what we can do." He crawled out of the cave and stood up, testing his injured ankle. It was numb and the numbness took away any pain he might have felt.

David hoped that the ice pack had refrozen while he slept. The open water distance, however, appeared larger than before. Perhaps Richard was looking for him. David reached into his suit and found a small flashlight. He began sweeping the light back and forth hoping to attract attention. "Come on Richard," he whispered. Fifteen minutes went by without a flicker of hope.

David crawled back into the ice cave. It was warm there compared to the icy outside. He was frustrated. There seemed to be no way out of this situation. He closed his eyes, lowered his head, and began to pray.

Now he found he wasn't on ice anymore. It was warm and dry and he was in a bed. His eyes scanned the room, trying to make sense of where he was. It looked like any other hospital room. There was a privacy curtain with its curved curtain rod and a typical antiseptic smell.

He was jarred back into reality when he heard a high-pitched voice say, "I think he is awake." Followed by another voice repeat, "... he is awake."

He opened his eyes to see two, rather small individuals standing just outside the doorway. "How are you?" asked the taller of the two.

"How are you?" repeated the shorter one.

CHAPTER 2

"This has to be a dream," David said out loud. The taller of the two individuals walked to the foot of the bed and said in a singsong cadence, "It may seem like a dream but what you feel is real."... "feel is real," repeated the smaller one, peeking out from behind her partner.

It didn't take David long to realize that this was not a dream and these childlike individuals were not children. "Where am I," he asked, "and who are you?"

The taller of the two ignored his question, she stepped forward and said, "I can tell you are feeling well." The shorter one stayed back and repeated, "feeling well."

"I don't know who you are or where I am," said David. "But I need to contact my family."

"It may sound bold, but all the people that need to know have been told." "Have been told," came the expected response.

"How could you notify anyone? You don't even know who I am!"

"Do not fear David, we know why you came and how you got here."

"... and how you got here." again repeated the little one.

A perplexed look came over David's face. His mind raced, trying to make sense of his predicament. "I must've slipped up, how else could they know my name? I must've had some sort of identification on me," he thought. He knew that was impossible; he had been on too many missions to make a rookie mistake like that.

"We found you nearly frozen, floating on a small iceberg. Thank goodness your dogs kept you warm,"... "kept you warm," interrupted the shorter one. "... or you might have died," the taller one said, finishing her sentence as she glanced back at her partner. The shorter one struggled to repeat her partner's words, her face flushed with embarrassment.

"My name is Rhymie and her name is Echo."

"My name is Echo," said the timid one.

"Echo, you have been named appropriately," said David. Echo smiled but did not reply.

David sat up in bed, his face more relaxed and thought,"They are kind of cute."

He had to be careful not to let his guard down. The situation was still not clear to him, "Who are these people? And where am I? These small beds would fit these two but not a big man like himself. This must be a children's hospital, but that makes no sense at all," he thought.

"What is this place?"

"It's the place you came looking for."... "came looking for."

"And that is?"

"It's where we live."... "where we live."

"Are there many that live here?"

"Oh yes, there are many that live here."... "that live here."

"Are they all like you, about the same size?"

"All except two."... "except two."

"Are they adults?"

"Yes."... "Yes."

"Are they your parents?"

The two burst into laughter as if that was the funniest thing they ever heard.

"You think we are children, but we are not," Rhymie giggled. Echo could not even echo, she was so amused.

"Well then what are you?"

Rhymie backed away from the bed, as did Echo. The two began whispering to each other in an animated way. They glanced back at David and then continued their discussion.

David sat up higher so that he could look out of the window. He saw several buildings, some stone and some brick. He couldn't see the street but he estimated the buildings were two or three stories high.

Rhymie and Echo told him that he was, in their words, "the place he came looking for." That was impossible, the place he was looking for was in the Arctic. There are no buildings in the Arctic, only ice and snow.

Could he have drifted far enough to reach Siberia? That didn't seem possible. It was thought that the Soviets did construct bases in Siberia for their secret work. Besides, Siberia is hundreds of miles from the North Pole.

"Okay, let's start from the beginning," he called to the pair.

They stopped talking, slowly turned and walked back toward David.

"You said you know about me, so how did you come to obtain that information?"

We know about everyone." ... "everyone."

David was frustrated. It seems that for every question he asked, he would get not just one ambiguous answer but two. Finally, he asked the question that changed the mood in the room.

"What is the name of the person in charge?" he asked in the most demanding voice he could muster.

The pair backed away and quickly moved to just outside the doorway where they began another excited discussion. David forced himself to sound angry "I want an answer and I want it now." He felt guilty having to be forceful with them. They were sweet and childlike.

As Rhymie and Echo walked back towards him, Echo tried to hide herself behind her larger companion. Both of them avoiding eye contact.

"Well, are you going to give me an answer?" he asked in a more gentle tone.

Rhymie stood with her head down while tapping her left foot on the floor. It was then when David noticed their clothing and especially their shoes! Their shoes! They were kind of pointy and curled up, much like what Elves might wear. Elves?? No, what kind of silly thought was that?

"Get a grip David. Elves?" he laughed to himself. "Of course they're dressed up like elves, it's Christmas time."

"I want an answer," he repeated a bit more impatiently.

"We...we are afraid to tell you." Echo did not repeat Rhymie's words.

"Why?"

"Because you won't believe us."..." believe us."

"Try me."

"We have to go now." They spun around and ran towards the door. Someone will come and talk to you soon." ..."soon."

"Wait! He called. David tried to stand up, but as soon as he did the room started to spin. The pain in his ankle convinced him to quickly retreat to the bed. He was not ready to chase them. His ordeal had apparently taken much of his strength. He felt woozy, the feeling you get when you sometimes stand up too quickly. David laid back down and the feeling of nausea came over him. He fought as hard as he could; he did not want to lose control.

"Come on David, show some character," he thought. It took a few minutes before the feeling of nausea passed. He needed to stay awake. He needed to find out more about where he was and who these people are.

When he regained his composure, he sat up in bed, and once again tried to learn as much as possible about his situation. He retested his ankle by putting some weight on it. It was painful but he took a few steps.

He made it to the hallway, but the throbbing of his lower leg was too much to bear. He struggled to get back to bed. He laid down, closed his eyes, and wondered what circumstances lay ahead.

CHAPTER 3

David tried to stay awake but soon fell asleep. He was lying on his side when he felt someone or something shaking his shoulder. A gruff voice woke him with a loud "Wake up! Wake up!" He opened his eyes to see four slightly larger versions of Rhymie and Echo. They appeared to be male, three with goatee style beards. He tried to wipe away the sleepiness by rubbing his eyes with his fingertips.

"You frightened Rhymie and Echo, the two who nursed you back to health. If it hadn't been for them you wouldn't be here now," the apparent leader said.

"You should be ashamed of yourself," another added.

"It always amazes me how you big people can be so mean," said the clean shaven one.

David was baffled by the words, "big people." He continued to rub his eyes with the knuckle of his right hand while looking at the four standing beside his bed. He could now see their ears...they were kind of pointy...like elves! He did not see that on Rhymie or Echo because they both had hair that covered their ears. "Is this possible? Am I dreaming this, or is this really happening?" David thought that this situation was getting to be very bizarre. He wanted to start getting some answers that made sense.

"Okay, you seem to know who I am but who are..." He was interrupted by the leader, who said, "Yes, we know who you are. We are not happy that you are here and we want you to leave as soon as possible."

"I would like to leave," he answered. "Just how do I do that?"

"And don't come back," said the one who had not spoken yet.

Obviously they didn't want David there and now his curiosity was rising.

"What are you hiding here that you don't want me to see?"

"Your presence will only cause trouble. We only want to be left alone," said the leader.

"We're different from you, we don't want and we don't need outsiders," said one of the four in a quiet voice.

"I see we have an unexpected visitor," said a voice from the doorway.

David and the other four turned to see a normal sized woman walking into the room. She was an attractive lady, her graying hair was done up in a bun and she wore a muted red dress with a white apron. Her smile and her voice were warm and friendly. She instantly reminded him of what his beloved grandmother might have looked like in her younger years.

"I believe David is confused and needs some sort of explanation about what has happened to him," she said. "He's our guest and he should be treated with respect. Don't you agree?"

All four of them bowed their heads and said, "Yes Mrs. C."

"Now excuse us, I wish to talk to our guest alone."

"But Mrs. C," they pleaded.

"Trust me, my dears."

"No Mrs. C, what if he tells? He's an outsider, what if he tells others?"

"And you think anyone will believe the tale he will tell? Surely we want to know why he undertook this dangerous journey in the dead of winter."

All four nodded in agreement, but still protested, "Don't tell anything of our secrets Mrs. C, please."

"Now you must know that I checked Mr. C's Big Book and we both agree that David is held in the highest regard and can be trusted. You also know that my time is very valuable and you must have some last-minute chores to do yourselves. Now get!"

David's mind was churning. Mr. and Mrs. C must be the two normal sized people that Rhymie and Echo told him about. But what secrets so worried the small ones? In the back of his mind, there was an ember of a thought that would not go away. The shoes, the ears, Mrs. C, the Big Book, could it be... It wasn't possible.

"Let's talk about what happened to you and how you came to us," said Mrs. C.

"I'd like that very much," David answered. "I have many questions."

She smiled and replied, "And your questions will be answered at the proper time."

She took his hands between both of hers, they were warm and her grip was firm. "I see your body temperature is back to normal. You are a very lucky person. You needed our help and we were glad to give it to you. Otherwise you would not have found us."

"We would've found you Mrs. C, we have the most modern equipment there is," he said.

Mrs. C smiled and said, "Perhaps all things are not what they seem to be."

"What does she mean by that?" he wondered.

David was concerned about the other team. He reasoned that if the small people or Mrs. C knew about him, they probably knew about the others.

"There were others working with me, do you know about them and are they safe?"

"I can assure you they are safe. The seaquake did not separate him as it did you and they were not thrown into the water as you were. They also know that you are safe and you will be returning to them as soon as the storm has passed."

"Seaquake, I thought it might be something like that," he replied.

"It was unfortunate, some of our people were being too protective."

David's expression changed, she seemed to indicate that somehow they caused the seaquake.

"You mean to say that you had something to do with the seaquake?"

"Our people are very protective."

"No person has the power to cause an earthquake," he answered.

"Power can come in many forms David."

David was confused by Mrs. C; he was still not sure who or what he was dealing with. The questions kept mounting; the earthquake or seaquake was something that no human could control. So much of what he heard didn't make sense. If this is a dream it was the most realistic dream David ever experienced. Could they have given him a hallucinogenic drug?

"Tell me Mrs. C, why are you among these rather unusual people, in the middle of the Arctic?"

"That will be answered in due time David, in due time."

David wondered why she was stalling. What was she hiding and why was she hiding it?

"You know Mrs. C, I don't have any idea where I am or how I got here."

"You are here with us, and you are safe. Some of our helpers brought you here," she said avoiding a straight answer.

"Does my family know where I am and that I am safe?" he asked.

"Yes, they know you are safe and that you will be home in a few days."

David's mind was in turmoil. He had countless numbers of questions he was trying to sort out. Mrs. C stood up, reached over, and gave him a big hug.

"I need to be someplace in a few minutes David. Someone will be here soon as I leave and will answer your questions."

"Will I see you again?" he asked.

As she was leaving the room she turned and replied with a cryptic response, "You will see me and another person."

"Wait." he called to her, "I don't understand."

She answered back, her voice trailing off as she hurried away, "It will become clear by the time you leave."

CHAPTER 4

Within minutes a tiny girl walked into the room with a tray of food. David sat up when he realized that she was not one of the small people he already met. She was even smaller than they were. Rhymie and Echo were probably the size of eighth-graders, while this tiny girl was sized more like his second grade daughter. She was almost lost under the heavy tray, but carried it effortlessly.

"Hello David, I'll bet you're hungry," she said as she placed the tray down on the table. David was surprised that she spoke in a manner that was unusual for her appearance.

"Yes, I'm very hungry. I don't think I have eaten in a while."

"Three days to be exact," she said.

The tiny girl had sandy colored hair, a round face and green eyes. She sounded like an adult, but did not look like one.

She placed a plate on a tray in front of David. The smell of eggs and toast made his mouth water and he quickly began eating. "You must have read my mind, this is exactly what I would've ordered," he said, taking a sip of coffee.

"Three days," David thought to himself. "It must be around December 24, another year away from home at Christmas time."

When he finished eating, the little girl removed the tray and placed it on a small nightstand. "Getting you home for Christmas will be a problem for us. We are very busy this time of year and I know you'll understand," she said. David was stunned, "Could this little girl read his mind?" he wondered.

"May I ask your name?"

"My name is Meghan."

"Meghan, almost everyone that I met here are different from the people in my hometown. Rhymie and Echo, and the four men that I met earlier, they all seem to be alike. But you look different and you have a gracious demeanor that goes beyond your appearance. Do you understand the word demeanor?"

"Yes, David, I understand that you view me as a small child. You believe that I am incapable of doing what I'm doing. I am not speaking or relating in a way that you would expect from a small child."

"I mean no disrespect," he stuttered.

"And honestly, none taken," she answered. "Things here are not always as they seem; this is a special place."

"Let's talk about this place. The people are different from where I call home. And yet this place shouldn't even exist. I looked out the window and saw buildings when I should only see ice and snow. What country built this place?"

Meghan smiled, "I can answer your questions and I know of your concerns, but it's probably better for you to see what we have here. This is a place, one that you could envision as a small child. Now you are an adult and you have an adult mind that would have difficulty accepting the answers I would give you. It will all become clear to you in time."

David's mind went on alert. She wouldn't or couldn't tell him what country built this place. Was he in danger now? Was he at some sort of secret place?"

This is ridiculous. Who could build a base so secret that it was only discovered by the new technology of satellites? Outer space? Aliens? "I better get control of myself," he thought.

Once again David turned to Meghan and asked, "Am I in danger?"

In a very gentle way she answered, "You can feel safe and secure with me, with all of us. You are in no danger, and you will be home soon. I promise."

David was comforted by her presence and words.

"David, we're running out of time. I will be back in a few minutes and many of your questions will be answered."

"Running out of time for what?" he called to her as she left the room.

"We're running out of time," he repeated her words. "Many of my questions will be answered," he said out loud. He wondered if she was just stalling, another way to keep him from getting the answers he needed. He still didn't know where he was, it was like a hospital but then again it wasn't.

It was time for David to take matters into his own hands. He knew that he would have a difficult time walking on his injured ankle. But staying in the room was no longer an option. He needed to explore and find the answers for himself.

He swung his feet over the side of the bed but somehow slipped between the two mattresses that had been pushed together to make his bed. He fell straight to the floor just as Meghan and a fellow named Quick Lee walked into the room. Quick Lee was pushing a cart that had a chair sitting on it.

Meghan laughed, "I see you tried to escape."

David attempted to hide his embarrassment by laughing with her. "Yes, as you can see, I'm not very good at it. I guess I need more practice."

They helped David to his feet and insisted that he sit on the chair they had tied down to the cart, making it a makeshift wheelchair. David thanked Meghan and Quick Lee for assisting him. Quick Lee said, "You're welcome," and something else that was far too fast for David to understand, so he just smiled and nodded yes.

"I'd like to try to walk," he said.

"We haven't much time and we have a long way to go," Meghan gently insisted.

"Where are we going?" asked David.

"To answer your questions," she answered.

CHAPTER 5

Meghan and Quick Lee tenderly assisted David onto the makeshift "wheelchair" and began a headlong race to somewhere. Quick Lee was pushing the cart as fast as he was able, and Meghan was somehow keeping pace. She was racing alongside where David was sitting. "Don't you think we should slowdown?" David asked, holding on for dear life. "I can see why you got Quick Lee to help you," David whispered to Meghan.

"I suppose he has a brother named Speedy," David added.

Meghan giggled and said, "Very funny David, no, but he does have a sister whose name is Swift Lee. We do have a Speedy but they are not related."

"This must be very important for us to be going this fast," David called out.

"You bet your life this is important," said Quick Lee. "I've never missed this event!"

David knew the type of answer he would get to his next question, "Where are we going?"

"You'll see when we get there," answered Meghan.

As they raced down the corridor, David was able to get a brief look into a few of the rooms. He determined it was not really a hospital but more like a health center. Like the room he was in, each had two undersized beds and two chairs.

When they came to an intersection, the nature of the building changed. The rooms now seemed more like a college dorm. They passed a large room that could have been a cafeteria with many tables and also what might have been a serving line. Yet with all the rooms and hallways they passed, they did not see another soul.

Finally they came to rest in front of a large picture window. "Just in time," said Meghan. "Not a minute to spare," added Quick Lee.

David leaned forward, trying to see what necessitated the rush to get there. It was dark, but with the flickering of the Aurora Borealis he got the impression that he was looking out into a courtyard of some size. He could see the outlines of adjoining buildings as well as those across from him.

Although the light was dim, David could see that there were a large number of individuals in the courtyard. He was sure that some sort of event was about to happen. He was more interested in finding out what this place was and why it was here.

"Okay, where are my answers?" David asked. Off in the distance the sound of a very large bell began chiming.

ONE," cried the crowd in unison.

At the same instant, across the courtyard a lone building became illuminated. At the very top of the tower David could see the outline of a large bell rocking back and forth announcing the time.

"TWO," again cried the group.

It's midnight, Christmas Day, in one small part of the world," said Meghan.

"THREE," announced the crowd. With each chime the volume increased. David turned his head and was about to ask Meghan what was happening when the scene became illuminated.

"FOUR." A huge Christmas tree, adorned with thousands of dazzling lights lit up the center of the courtyard, with dozens of smaller trees around the perimeter.

"FIVE." Four moving spotlights danced on the ornamentation that adorned the large tree, making it an amazing sight.

"SIX." The moving reflections of light and shadows illuminated the crowd that filled the square.

"SEVEN." The glorious blaze of light and the cheering of the crowd made the hair on the back of David's neck tingle.

"EIGHT." Three more spotlights, one green, one blue and one red began scanning the buildings in an impressive display of colors.

"NINE." There was electricity in the air, the anticipation that something big was about to happen.

"TEN." The scene then went dark, except for one building. This building had a huge door that slowly began to swing open.

David realized that this was probably the big event he expected. He watched closely and saw emerging from the doorway were two horses, and then another two horses, no...wait they're not horses, they're reindeer! And then there was another pair and still another pair. It was in fact eight reindeer pulling a sleigh! And there was a bearded man dressed in red sitting in the sleigh.

"ELEVEN."

And then..."Is that him, Santa?" questioned David. He was startled, what was he seeing? Was he hallucinating, was he still in the freezing Arctic water or was this really happening? No, this was a pageant, a parade, a show, a celebration of Christmas. This cannot be the real thing. Santa and his sleigh? There is no such thing. Ridiculous.

"MIDNIGHT."

When the bell struck 12, the face of the clock glowed, outlining the Roman numeral XII. Both clocked hands pointed upward. The crescendo of sound from the crowd was at its peak.

Meghan looked up to David and shouted, "You look skeptical; you don't believe what you see with your very own eyes."

"It's quite spectacular, you might see this type of show in Vegas. It's really quite impressive," David yelled.

"The bell you heard marked the stroke of midnight in one small part of the world. Now this is the time for Santa to begin delivering gifts to those who believe," Meghan shouted into David's ear.

Quick Lee chimed in with, "Just wait a second and you'll see something that you will never forget for the rest of your life."

David, still in denial said, "Yeah, I'm sure I'll see those reindeer fly."

Once again there came a huge roar from the crowd, as a person, a woman, climbed the stairs to the platform that held the reindeer, the sleigh, and a person dressed in a red suit trimmed in white. David was not sure. It was a long way off in the distance but to him it looked very much like Mrs. C.

"Meghan, is that Mrs. C, the lady I met earlier?" asked David.

"Yes, David that is Mrs. C, and she is married to Mr. C, who is sitting in the sleigh."

Mrs. C went to the front of the team of reindeer, pausing in front of each of them, patting them and giving each a treat. She reached the sleigh, leaned over to the man in the red suit and they exchanged hugs and kisses. She turned to face the crowd and both Mr. and Mrs. C waved to the crowd.

The excitement of the throng seemed to cause the reindeer to become restless and eager to move. Mrs. C moved away from the sleigh and Mr. C gave a gentle shake to the reins. Slowly the reindeer began to take short hops, gradually gaining speed and distance between each stride. The pace began to quicken. Effortlessly the team and sleigh began levitating, leaving the ground, gaining speed going higher and faster. They circled the area twice and then in a flash they disappeared into the night. David sat back in his chair, a look of bewilderment on his face, his mouth open, he looked at Meghan and asked, "Is this real, is this a dream, are you real?"

Meghan answered, "David, we know you are a man of faith. Trust your faith, this is real."

"Then the man in the red suit is, dare I say it, is the real Santa Claus?"

Both Meghan and Quick Lee smiled, reached over and gave David a hug.

A thousand thoughts and a thousand questions still filled David's mind. He thought of Clement Moore's timeless classic The Night Before Christmas and laughed, "The reindeer were actually prancing and pawing. Even if I pretend to believe this, he can't carry all the toys in that small sleigh."

Meghan smiled and said, "Christmas is magical and soon you will see how it all works."

David sat there, his fingers interlocked on the top of his head, looking out the window, watching the assembly, many of them dancing, and all of them seemed to be enjoying themselves. David was enthralled over what had just taken place.

"Meghan, I think you're right and there is a lot for me to learn. When do I begin my North Pole education?"

"How about right now," she answered.

CHAPTER 6

Meghan took David's hand, squeezed it, and said, "I know that what you're seeing is hard to believe. I understand that, but this is a very different place. A place with very different rules, rules that contradict the logic of where you come from."

"Meghan, I wish that I could believe what you are trying to tell me. It's very hard for me to understand. My mind tells me that what I see is not really happening," said David.

"If this is a dream, it's the most vivid dream I've ever had. If it's not a dream, then I must be going insane. I saw a man in a red suit with a team of reindeer seem to fly up into the air and then disappear into the night. Reindeer don't have wings, so in my mind, they can't fly and what I saw was an illusion, like a magic trick."

"I can't really convince you with words, but let's move on and maybe, just maybe, it might start to make sense to you," said Meghan.

"Let's start with a question that you'd like to have answered," she said.

"Am I really at the North Pole?"

"Yes, and that is Santa flying in his sleigh," she answered.

Quick Lee, who had been very quiet, chimed in, "You still have your doubts even though you have seen it with your own eyes?"

David's mind was in turmoil. Was he having hallucinations? Was this really happening? He knew that there were very powerful drugs with mind–altering effects. And yet he didn't seem to have any symptoms or sense any dreamlike conditions. In fact, he felt fine.

He gazed out the window watching the crowd, wondering how this place could have remained undetected. Speaking to no one in particular he said, "There have been explorers that have claimed to reach the North Pole. How could it be that they've never found this place?"

Quick Lee stroked his beard, looked David straight in the eye and said, "David, the magic of Christmas has protected us, not just a Christmastime, but all year round."

"But I'm here, it didn't protect you, I found you," David answered.

"You didn't find us David, we found you," said Meghan quietly.

"What is to prevent others from coming here?" asked David.

"Christmas magic," answered a voice from the doorway.

As Mrs. C walked into the room, her presence commanded attention. Quick Lee ran to get a chair for her, but she motioned for him to stop.

"David, when we saved you from your unfortunate accident, we could have arranged for you to be rescued by your companion. No one, including you or any of the others, would have discovered us. You would have reported that there was nothing really here, just a vast area of ice and snow," said Mrs. C.

"Accident? That was no accident; it was a force of nature. Accidents are the result of someone making a mistake," said David.

"Trust me David, it was an accident. Some of our elves tend to be over–protective," she answered.

"You're telling me that it was on purpose, a way of stopping me from discovering you and this place?"

"Yes, it just got a little out of hand and your heroics put you in danger. We tried to correct our mistakes but it was too late and it became a rescue mission," she said. "Now that you're here, we hope that you understand why it happened. It was not done to harm you but to confuse you, to send you off course so that you would not find us."

"We were very aware of the reason you and your group were sent here; to investigate what was here. And again I will tell you that you would not have found this place even with your technology. We also know of your character. When the accident occurred we decided that it was time for you to learn the truth about Santa Claus."

"Okay, let's assume that there is a Santa and this is the North Pole. Why tell me?" asked David.

"Many, many people do not believe in Santa Claus, they think it's all made up," replied Mrs. C. "There are many traditions that people have regarding Christmas, yet no one knows for sure how and why these traditions started. We think that as you learn about us, what we do and why we do it, you will find a way to pass this information on," she said.

"And how do you propose I do this?" he asked.

"Write a book," said Mrs. C. "Write about what has happened so far and what you will learn before you leave."

"Who's going to believe this?" asked David.

"The people who want to believe will believe." she answered. "If you write it as a fantasy adventure story, people will accept it for what it is: a story. You are here and yet you don't believe what you are seeing. How can you expect the readers to believe your story as fact?" she finished.

"But what if you're wrong and some people do try to find this place? That may cause some major problems," he said.

Mrs. C smiled and said, "We underestimated your technology, it was easy for us to detect airplanes and even a submarine that broke through the ice. But your satellites surprised us. We weren't aware that you were able to observe us. And those observations caused you to come looking for us. We have since taken measures to keep us hidden. Now we know that you have this capability and we won't let it happen again. We cannot afford to be discovered by people who are interested in making a profit. We have faith in you and trust that you will keep us safe and spread the spirit of Christmas."

David understood the importance of keeping the idea of Santa, his workshop, the elves and reindeer as a fantasy. If this was exposed to the public, the hordes of people who would attempt to reach this area would be disruptive and dangerous. This place would soon be inundated with hotels and restaurants and who knows what else.

"But I'm here, and you said earlier that I would soon be reunited with my family and the other team members. So how will your secret be kept?" asked David.

"This will be taken care of," said Mrs. C.

Before David could say another word, Meghan asked. "How would you like to learn the story of Mr. and Mrs. Claus?"

"Everyone knows the story of Santa," answered David.

"Really? So you know how he taught the reindeer how to fly? And how he got to the North Pole and found the elves?" Meghan answered.

"I see your point," David said sheepishly.

Mrs. C smiled, "We would like you to read a story to our very young elves and pixies. It's a history lesson that we would like to pass along."

Elves! Real elves! That was the first time that anyone here said that word and pixies too! What other wondrous creatures live here, he wondered. David was beginning to soften; to let his guard down. Perhaps there are many more things that he didn't understand.

"It sounds interesting and I'd be delighted," he answered.

"I think you will find it very rewarding," said Mrs. C.

David still wanted to get some answers about his rescue and how they thought they would be able to avoid future detection of this place. But a few minutes of reading a story to some of the elves and pixies could be enjoyable. It might give him more insight about these individuals and what their purposes were.

Quick Lee and Meghan began to push David's cart down the hallway in the opposite direction of the room that David had been in. With Meghan still at his side they entered a large room that could also be called an auditorium. At one end, there was a fireplace and a huge overstuffed sofa, with two loveseats and four armchairs. David hopped from the cart to the sofa, trying to keep his weight off of his sore ankle.

He sat in the room for a few minutes, enjoying the heat from the fireplace. Then two husky looking fellows came in pushing a cart that was carrying a very large, heavy book. Under Meghan's direction, they placed the cart directly behind David's sofa. The two elves then spun David's sofa around so now the fireplace was behind him. Now David was looking out into the auditorium. Row upon row of chairs filled the room. A semicircular balcony bordered by a white railing was beginning to fill with spectators.

From the doorway came the sounds of many excited individuals. In they came, elves and pixies, tiny, beautiful people, hopping and skipping into the room. They bounced on the sofa, some landing on David's lap. Others cuddled up to him wrapping their arms around his. Two climbed onto the back of the sofa and settled on his shoulders, their tiny legs dangling down with their tiny hands holding onto his ears for balance.

The room was quickly reaching capacity, with not only elves and pixies, but all manner of individuals in appearance and sizes. David sensed the excitement and electricity of the crowd. There was a feeling that another major event was about to happen.

David guessed that the pixies were the smallest of the group, and they were probably the ones that had settled on his shoulders. He thought they were the cutest collection of youngsters he had ever seen. He introduced himself and asked the names of those adorable cuties. Buttercup, Sports Guy, Smuggle, and Vroom were the names they gave. He thought Buttercup was a pixie, but the other three were probably young elves. Some were girls and some were boys that were too young to grow a beard.

Were there such things as adult pixies and teenage elves? There were others that did not fit the category of elf or pixie. Meghan was one of those that puzzled David. She didn't dress like an elf and seemed to be perhaps a bit too large to be a tiny pixie. He wondered if etiquette would be breached if he asked her in what category she was. He thought better of it and decided that now was not the right time.

Meghan zigzagged her way through the crowd and walked up to David and said, "By tradition, this book is only read after midnight on Christmas Eve."

"Well then it's Christmas, if it's after midnight," said David.

"That's correct. But it's only Christmas in one very small sliver of the earth," said Meghan.

David quickly surmised, "I see, we're at the North Pole. All the time zones meet here. So technically it's Christmas here."

Vroom, one of the young elves, voiced a very knowledgeable answer, "But for most of the world, it's still Christmas Eve."

"So Christmas magic will sweep across the earth, one time zone at a time," said David.

"We know it's Christmas now," said the pixie on David's left shoulder.

"Is Christmas Day when Christmas magic is the strongest?" asked David.

"Everyone knows that," said Smuggle with an attitude. David was now sure that Smuggle was an elf from his name and his mischievous answer and the brassiness he exhibited.

"Smuggle, you weren't very polite to our guest. I know you can do better," said Meghan in a caring tone. "I think you know what should happen next," she finished.

"I'm sorry for saying, everyone knows that," said Smuggle.

"It's okay Smuggle, there are a lot of things that I don't know," David answered.

"Can you read the story please?" said another of the small people.

"I can't wait," said Buttercup.
Off in the far corner of the room was Mrs. C. She tried to remain inconspicuous but she was very easy to spot in the group. Mrs. C nodded her head in approval. It was time to read a story.

CHAPTER 7

David was beginning to feel uncomfortable with the honor given to him. He was not sure why he was chosen to read this book. He waved toward Mrs. C trying to get her attention. He pointed to the book and then pointed to her, gesturing that she should be reading the book. Mrs. C was knitting something, she smiled, lifted up her knitting as if holding an imaginary book and then pointed back to David. He smiled and shook his head. He understood her message.

Meghan explained to David that the book contained a story, a history lesson about Santa Claus, Mrs. Claus and everything else associated with Christmas. The book can only be opened at midnight on Christmas Eve. More and more people came. The balcony was filling up with all sorts of different looking individuals. Many were sitting with their legs hanging over the edge, straddling the balusters, others were standing, and still others sitting on shoulders of those who were standing. It was a packed house.

From somewhere behind David, a loud booming voice called out, "QUIET DOWN." David turned around, looked over his shoulder, and saw a lady elf.

Meghan whispered to David, "I hope you know what a roast is."

He whispered back, "Yes, I do and I hope I can handle it."

The lady elf walked down where David was sitting. "YOU ALL KNOW ME, MY NAME IS LOTTIE AND I KNOW THAT SOME OF YOU CALL ME LOUD LOTTIE.

The crowd laughed and applauded. Lottie reached over and put her arm around David's neck, and gave him a hug. "I WANT TO INTRODUCE OUR READER FOR TODAY."

"HIS NAME IS DAVID AND HE COMES TO US UNEXPECTEDLY. HE THOUGHT HE WAS LOOKING FOR US, BUT WE HAD TO GO LOOKING FOR HIM. HE IS PART OF AN INTELLIGENCE AGENCY. BUT HE MUST NOT HAVE TOO MUCH INTELLIGENCE, CROSSING THE ARCTIC IN THE COLDEST POSSIBLE TIME WITH A DOGSLED."

David laughed along with the crowd.

"WE FOUND HIM IN AN ICE CAVE WITH NO FOOD, NO WATER, NO HEAT, NO LIGHT, AND NO HOPE. AND I'LL REPEAT IT AGAIN, HE IS PART OF THE UNITED STATES INTELLIGENCE AGENCY." Lottie jumped up and sat on David's lap. She then gave him a kiss on the cheek and said, "ISN'T HE CUTE?"

"Someone in the crowd yelled, "He's blushing." Once again the crowd roared.

"WELL, LET'S SEE IF HE KNOWS HOW TO READ. LET'S GIVE A WARM SANTA'S WORKSHOP ROUND OF APPLAUSE FOR OUR GUEST, DAVID."

In spite of his sore leg, David stood up, looked at the crowd waved and blew kisses to the crowd. "Thank you, thank you, and I think you're kind of cute too Lottie."

She blushed and quietly said, "Thank you."

Two elves pushed a cart that held the large book and positioned it in front of David. Another elf brought a stool that David could sit on and take the pressure off of his painful leg.

The cover of the book was very large in size and heavy in weight. It was adorned with Christmas illustrations depicting a Christmas Star, a manger, reindeer, sleighs, Christmas trees, and stockings that circled the title.

The words _Santa_, _Sarah,_ and _Genesis_ were spelled out in gold leaf snowflakes. The title gave David some clue as to the contents of the book. He reached over, using both hands, and lifted the heavy cover opening the book to the first chapter. It read, "Chapter 1 The Beginning."

The pages of the book were also inlayed in gold leaf. The first page contained an illustration of a man and a dog walking on a spring day. The trees were in full bloom, a fusion of colors illuminated by a bright sun.

The sketch gave the impression of a windy day, with tree limbs bending because of a hefty breeze.

The man in the painting was carrying what appeared to be a mailbag. The dog, walking alongside the man, was a golden lab. The bright sunlight, filtered by the flowers and the leaves, created shadows and added colors to the scene. David thought that the artist did a magnificent job; the painting almost seemed to be alive.

David cleared his throat, and began reading:

"CHAPTER ONE – THE BEGINNING"

"Kris Kringle was the post man for the small village of Nicholas. Each afternoon Kris and his dog Casey would deliver the mail to the town's inhabitants."

David began reading the next sentence of the story when he was interrupted by a rush of sounds from the audience. Gasps, laughter, and applause filled the arena. David looked up trying to see what caused the outburst. His face assumed a puzzled expression; he then looked towards the audience to where Mrs. C was sitting. He found her smiling and shaking her head in a positive way. He looked back at the page and something caught his attention, something on the page was different.

It was the painting, something in the painting had moved, something flickered. It appeared that a flower petal skittered across in front of the dog, another petal gently swung to and fro as it was falling to the ground. More and more objects appeared to take life.

Slowly, almost imperceptibly, the painting of the man was moving. His head was starting to curl upward. He was leaning forward, straining, pulling his neck and shoulders, peeling away from the paper. Slowly his arms became detached from the page and eventually his entire body rose and was standing up, like a paper cutout doll. And while this was happening, the dog, the trees, the mailbox and all the other items were straining, pulling hard to detach themselves from the page.

Bit by bit, the scene changed, the characters were no longer flat cutouts. They became three-dimensional, alive and they, like actors on stage took over the narration. David once again looked over to see Mrs. C's reaction; she was smiling in approval of what was taking place. He sat back, folded his arms across his chest, relaxed, and became a spectator.

"Casey, come along," Kris said to his dog. Casey would accompany Kris as he made his daily deliveries, sniffing each mailbox to see who had visited last. Along the way he would stop and talk to the people he met, discussing the events of the day.

"Casey would bark if they were lingering too long while talking to someone. Kris would laugh and excuse himself from the conversation. He would pat his companion on the head and say, "Casey, I

think you know our time schedule better than I do."

At that moment, with the exception of Casey the dog, the scene froze... Casey, her tail still wagging looked out at the audience and began to speak, "Christmas is the only time of year that I can speak. This is the story of my family, Kris and Sarah Kringle and how they became Mr. and Mrs. Santa Claus. I know the story very well because I was there when it happened."

The crowd burst into cheers and laughter. David stood up laughing and clapping along with the crowd. As the applause died down, David sat down and was about to resume telling the story. He was interrupted as the voice resumed the narration and the painting once again became alive. David sat back and again became a member of the audience while the book read itself.

The man in the painting begin to speak, *"Casey, there are some people in this town that don't have a lot. I can tell by looking at their clotheslines that some people are struggling to make ends meet. I wish there was a way that we could help them,"* he said. *Casey looked up at Kris, raised one ear and barked her approval.*

"Look over at that house," he said, where Margie and Julia live. Some of their clothes on the clothesline look ragged. I know Mr. Emmett has had a string of bad luck, he hurt his back and has been unable to work. I'm sure they have enough

food to eat but money is probably a problem and it looks like the children's clothing needs replacing."

The man and his dog continued on their mail route; Kris was making mental notes of which families could use some kind of assistance. Some families outwardly seemed to be doing well while others showed varying degrees of lacking the necessities.

After Kris finished his mail route he went back to the post office, closed up shop, and then headed for home.

As they approached home they knew that Sarah was cooking dinner. The aroma made both Kris and Casey's mouth water. In fact everything Sarah cooked made their mouth water. Sarah was not a very large person, so when they hugged she was almost a full head shorter than Kris.

"How did your day go?" she asked.

"Fine," he replied.

Just by his short answer, Sarah knew that something wasn't quite right.

"Why don't you wash up? Dinner will be ready in a few minutes," she said.

As they ate dinner Kris was very quiet. Sarah was doing most of the talking.

"I went to the market this morning and met Mrs. Green. Her husband fell and broke his ankle," she said. "They've had a lot of bad luck lately," she finished.

Kris looked up from his plate, closed his eyes and said, "They have three children and he can't work, they'll have to cut back on things."

"And they can't cut too much," Sarah added.

Kris replied, "We passed their house on the way home, and the house could use some repairs. We need to find a way to help these people. I thought maybe I could volunteer and help repair the roof, but the shingles can be expensive and I know Mr. Green might be offended if we just try to give him the money. He's a very proud man of a very proud family."

"Maybe I can sew some clothing for the children," Sarah offered. "It's really the children that I am concerned about," she added.

Kris agreed, "Yes I worry about them and a couple of other families."

Kris and Sarah both loved children but for some reason they never had any of their own.

"Casey and I were walking down Mason Street, and I was looking at some houses when I noticed the clothesline in the Petersons backyard," said

Kris. *"It was easy to see that some of the clothes were not in very good condition."*

Sarah looked up at Kris and said, "They could use some help, that's for sure."

"I also saw some toys that the Gillard's had in their backyard," Kris said "Those boys and girls could use some new ones."

"There are a few families like that here in Nicholas," replied Sarah, running her fingers through her shoulder length hair. "So how can we help?" Sara asked.

Kris sat down in his favorite chair, crossed his legs, took a long deep breath, and said, "I know it sounds crazy but if I could make some toys and you could make some clothes we could donate them to these families."

"No, I don't think it's crazy. I've wanted to do something for those families for quite a while now," said Sarah, as she sat down on Kris's lap.

"I think I can do something for some of these children," said Kris. "I can make some toys in my workshop for some of the younger ones."

"I know some of the older children would appreciate some new clothes for school and special occasions," offered Sarah. "I'm willing to start sewing now. If you could give me a list of the children, I can make a pretty good guess as to

sizes they might wear. And for the others I don't know too well, scarves and socks would do just fine."

"Let's not let this get too big," said Kris, "I know you Sarah you will want to include a lot more."

"Can we make a list?" she said. "Then we can decide how much we would want to do."

"It will be easy making a list, there aren't that many and I can have it by tomorrow," he said. "I'm concerned that some of the parents of these children are proud people and may be offended by what they might feel is charity," Kris said.

"I'm sure we'll think of something, some way so that no one will need to feel offended," she said.

"I hope so," he said." Thank you."

"Thank you for what?" Sara questioned.

"Thank you for agreeing to do this. It will be a lot of work for you," Kris said.

"I think we will both feel good about this when it's completed, even if it's a lot of hard work for both of us," she answered.

Kris and Sarah were good people but the task they set for themselves was very difficult and almost never happened.

With that sentence, the characters, Kris, Sarah, and Casey the dog, melted back into a painting that marked the end of Chapter One.

The audience applauded, David looked over toward Meghan and whispered, "What do I do now?" Meghan smiled and replied, "Go on to the next chapter."

CHAPTER 8

David turned the page to the next chapter. This time the painting showed the inside of a log home. Kris was sitting on one side of the fireplace while Sarah sat opposite him. The burning logs were the only source of light in the room. Casey was sound asleep on the floor.

Before David could even begin reading, the flames in the fireplace began to flicker, and the characters once again began to move and soon became three-dimensional.

"CHAPTER TWO – THE LIST" said David.

As he began to speak, a narrator interrupted him. A confused look appeared on David's face but it quickly disappeared as he once again became a spectator.

"Okay, I've made a list of the children," said Kris, showing Sarah a large sheet of yellow paper. "This side has the names of the children I think would enjoy having a toy. The other side are those who might appreciate clothing. And these at the bottom are the names of those I'm not sure of." Sarah scanned the list as Kris watched her face for any sign that might reveal her feelings. Each time her eyebrows raised, Kris responded by

saying "what" or "who was that?" Sara kept reviewing the list, and ignored Chris's questions. "I can think of five or six children who are not on this list," she said.

"Not all of them need help," he replied.

"But you can't leave some out, how would that make them feel?"

"If we include these nine or ten children, it'll be nearly half of the children in the village."

"Yes it's a lot, so a few more would not be a problem."

Kris stood up, shook his head back and forth in disagreement, and said, "You're probably thinking we should do this for every child in the village?"

"Well let's consider it, how much more would it be?"

"Good Lord, it might take until Christmas to get it done."

Sarah put her finger on one of the names to hold her place on the list. She looked up at Kris with a quizzical look.

"What are you thinking about?" he asked.

"Great idea," said Sarah. "We could give the gifts as presents for Christmas."

"You're joking aren't you?" he asked.

"No, it's a way to celebrate, celebrate the birth of the Christ child. We have enough time to complete this by Christmas. A gift for every child."

"You are serious aren't you?"

"Let's at least think about it," she said.

The next day Kris made a list of every child in the village. As days went by, Sarah convinced Kris that it was possible. The idea of giving the gifts at Christmas intrigued Kris and he reluctantly agreed.

In a small village like Nicholas, it's not unusual for everyone to know everyone else. Kris, as the village's mailman, certainly knew the names and faces of each family. It was also not unusual for Sarah to walk with Kris and Casey while they were making their rounds. So when Sarah accompanied Kris more often than usual, no one really noticed. Nor did they notice that Sarah carried a small notepad and frequently scribbled notes, especially after seeing a child whose name was on the clothing list. Occasionally Kris would lean over and whisper something to her and she would quickly write in her notebook.

"I'm certain that we have the name of every child in this village," said Kris, checking his mail pouch to be sure he had delivered all the mail. "Well this

is quite a list," said Sarah, looking at her notepad. "It will take us until Christmas."

Kris put his arm around his wife, squeezed her close and quietly said, "We can't go halfway, I don't know what we would do with 32 shirts and 21 sweaters of all different sizes, and none of them will fit you or I." Sarah laughed and added, "We start tonight."

When they arrived home, Kris helped Sarah prepare dinner. Since they were together the entire afternoon, she was glad to have his help. Kris could cook, but as he liked to say, "My cooking while you are watching would be like Rembrandt mixing the paint and his assistant doing the painting." Kris set the table, washed and cut up the potatoes and beets, and filled the teakettle. He then excused himself to his workshop.

He was an avid woodworker, and sometimes fantasized about making his living working with wood. But he knew that his position of mailman was quite secure and he was wary of quitting his position. Surely he never wanted to endanger his comfortable life with Sarah. He went to his workshop to check his wood and paint supplies. As he estimated the supplies needed, the time to create, assemble and paint the toys he planned to make. He became very concerned about the enormity of the task.

"DINNER," called Sarah, breaking his trance. "I'll be right there," he called back.

When dinner was finished, Kris took the dishes, silverware, and cups to the sink, washed them, and set them aside to dry. After he finished, he came back to the table, sat down, reached across the table and took both of Sarah's hands. "I'm not sure we can do this." he said.

Sarah, a surprised look on her face asked, "Why, what happened?"

"It's too much, we can't get it done, and asking you to do all that knitting and sewing, it's impossible," he said.

"Hard work is something many people try to avoid. Hard work will make you stronger and I don't have any problem with hard work," she answered.

"Honey, I know that we both can do hard work, but it's just too much, we don't have enough time."

Sarah stood up and said, "I'll be right back."

She went to the bedroom and came back with seven pieces of paper. She laid them down in front of Kris. "

"I've broken it down by month. This first piece of paper lists what I need to accomplish this month. As you can see, I'm knitting scarves and hats. I don't have to worry about sizes. I can make enough each month and have plenty of time left over. When we get closer I will make some special items for those in need."

"It's a lot of work, but is it worth it?" asked Kris.

"Okay Mr. Kringle, I'll agree with you. It's a lot of work, but do I think it's worth it? Yes, it's worth it. We're helping people. The part I think is most important, is that this is a way to celebrate the birth of the Christ child."

"Well Mrs. Kringle, I can see that you really, really want to complete this project. I will carry out my part of it. If you can do it, I can too. You really are a strong woman."

Sarah smiled, went to Kris and gave him a big hug and said, "When we finish this project, I know we both will be very happy."

CHAPTER 9

David was well aware that all he needed to do was to announce the chapter name and the chapter number:

"CHAPTER THREE – CHRISTMAS EVE"

The chill of November reminded both Sarah and Kris that Christmas was not far away. Yet to be decided was how the gifts would be distributed.

"I can only see one way to do this. We will have to deliver the presents after dark, in the middle of the night," said Sarah.

"To each house?" asked Kris.

"Yes, if we're going to be anonymous, what other way could there be?" answered Sarah.

"So that the children will have gift on Christmas morning," said Kris.

"Exactly," she replied.

"What if we took the presents Christmas Eve and put them all in the gazebo where people would see them Christmas morning?" Kris replied.

"I think it might be a circus, people pawing through the packages looking for their names.

And remember, not all of them will be getting gifts," said Sarah.

"So we have to go to almost every single house in town in the middle of the night?" asked Kris.

"Yes, unless you have a better idea," said Sarah.

"No, I'm afraid you're right," he said.

The remaining few weeks went by quickly and though it was difficult, both Kris and Sarah were able to complete the task of providing gifts for every child in their small village. But the nagging question that Kris had was, "What about the people who did not have children living in their house. It seemed unfair that they would be left out."

With less than two weeks before Christmas, he asked Sarah, "What are we going to do about the other families, the ones without children?"

"That's easy," she said. "We will give them a Christmas greeting note."

"Christmas greeting note, what is a Christmas greeting note?" questioned Kris.

"A Christmas greeting note is just a piece of paper that carries a message celebrating the birth of Jesus Christ," she answered.

"Where did you learn of this?" asked Kris.

"I just invented it," said Sarah with a laugh.

"Are you serious, are you really thinking of us doing that?" asked Kris again.

"Do you have a better idea?" replied Sarah.

"What kind of message are you thinking about?"

"Well, I thought we could make some potato prints of things like the Christmas star, or a manger or other things that are associated with Christmas."

"Potato prints, what are potato prints? I've never heard of them."

"Let me show you," she said. Sarah went to the cupboard, pulled out a potato and cut it lengthwise. She then took a star shaped cookie cutter, and pressed it into the newly cut face of the potato. Then with a knife, she trimmed around the shape of the star leaving it so that it was raised on the flat cut side of the potato.

"Oh I see," said Kris. "So now you use ink or paint to cover the star and use it like a stamp. What a great idea."

Sarah smiled and said, "I know you are artistic enough to carve three or four different Christmas designs. We'll stamp the prints on paper and add a message."

"What kind of message are you thinking about?"

"Oh, maybe something simple like 'Merry Christmas' or 'Wishing you a Jolly Christmas'," said Sarah. "Be creative, it is just a way of acknowledging those families who will not have a gift delivered."

"This sounds like fun," said Kris. "I'll get started right now."

Kris created four different potato stamps within an hour. It took him a few hours more to create a potato stamp that carried the message, "Merry Christmas." He also created another "Merry Christmas" stamp, this one in cursive.

With all the gifts ready to be wrapped, Kris used the potato stamps to make the wrapping paper more attractive. He randomly placed stars on the paper and created another potato stamp depicting holly leaves with red berries. In addition, he created a stamp that would help identify who was to receive that gift.

For a

Special Child

Sarah wrapped the presents and would write the name of the child underneath the stamp Kris created.

As Kris began stamping the Christmas notes, he found that the flimsy paper was just not right. It was missing something, perhaps it lacked

74

character or appeal. He remembered that he had some thicker, heavier stock. It was similar to what playing cards were made of. It was used to separate some of the post office supplies he had received just a few days ago. It was perfect for the task. He printed out two or three of the Christmas greeting notes and showed them to Sarah.

"What do you think of these?"

"Yes, these look much better. Let's call them Christmas cards," she said.

Two days before Christmas Eve, everything was ready. The gifts were wrapped and addressed as well as the Christmas cards.

After dinner that evening, Sarah said to Kris, "Close your eyes and don't peek." Sarah went into the back bedroom and brought out some clothes, she stood in front of Kris and said, "Open your eyes."

"What in the world is this?"

"This is your disguise," she said.

She was holding a bright red jacket adorned with a white furry collar and cuffs with matching pants and hat.

"Wow, this will draw a lot of attention," he said.

"Do you think if anyone from the village saw someone dressed like this they would ever think it was you?" asked Sarah.

"No, I probably am the last person they would ever guess it was," he said. "But they might be able to see my face."

"Not if you wear this," she said handing him what looked like a ball of cotton. "It's your beard, your white fluffy beard, no one will be able see your face."

Sarah helped Kris put on his beard then stood back and laughed. She held up a mirror so that Kris could see himself. Both of them laughed happily.

"Since we are going in the middle of the night, I doubt that anyone will see us, if they do see us, they'll never guess that it's you and I," she said.

"Us, you mean you've got the same suit as I do?" he asked.

"No, there's not enough material to make one like yours. I'll think of something" she added.

Kris tried on the jacket and the pants and said, "These are way too big."

Sarah went into the bedroom, and brought out a big pillow, and said, "Use this pillow to help fill you out."

Kris struggled to push the pillow down into his pants and under his red jacket.

"Yes, this is one more reason why no one will ever think it's me," he said.

"But you Sarah, you'll need some kind disguise. Maybe they won't be able to tell it's me but you need some sort of disguise too."

"I'll have something, don't you worry," said Sarah.

Finally, the day came! Christmas Eve was finally here! It was by all aspects a typical day, their normal routine was in fact routine. But once suppertime came, both Kris and Sarah were excited and apprehensive at the same time. Was this the best idea that they ever had or was it the silliest thing they ever attempted?

Just before midnight, Kris put on his red pants. He had a bit of a problem tucking the pillow into position. After a few tucks and pulls he eventually managed to get his belt buckle latched. He put on his red jacket with the white furry cuffs. Sarah helped him button his jacket and placed his red hat with furry white trimmings on his head. She then placed his white cotton beard into position. She stepped back and asked Kris to turn around so that she could see that everything was in its proper place. "No one can tell it's you, because I can't tell it's you," she laughed.

*"I just hope I'll be able to sit down in the wagon,"
he said.*

*Kris walked, perhaps waddled, from the cabin to
the shed where his stallion, Old Billy was waiting.
A light misty rain was falling, a change from the
ice pellets that fell earlier in the day.*

*"Well Billy, I'll bet you never thought we'd be
doing this. It's going to be late, it's going to be
cold and it's going to be long. I hope you're ready
for this."*

*He placed a hat with a large brim on Billy's head
to protect him from the ice pellets that might fall
as the evening got colder. Kris also put a blanket
on Billy's back to help keep him warm and dry.*

*The cart was packed, the wagon was hitched, and
everything was ready to go.*

*Just then a figure appeared in the doorway.
Casey could not make out who the stranger was
and let out a loud "**Woof**." "Shhhh.... Quiet Casey,
you'll wake up the neighbors," said the very
familiar voice of Sarah. She was dressed in a
costume similar to Kris's, but it didn't have the
same color or trimmings. Instead, it was complete
with a hat and a rather plump tummy.*

*"I thought that you didn't have enough material
to make a suit for yourself," said Kris.*

*Sarah hopped onto the wagon and said, "I didn't
have enough of the material that I used for your*

suit. But I had enough of a different color to make one for myself. It's a lighter red, almost a pink, but in the dark no one will be able to tell."

"They still can see your face," said Kris.

"Oh no they won't," said Sarah, putting on a white cotton beard just like the one that Kris wore.

Kris adjusted his beard and tried to give Sarah kiss. It was impossible, the thick cotton provided a barrier. Both of them burst into laughter.

"Oh don't we make a pair," said Kris. "Giddy up Billy, it's time to deliver our Christmas gifts," said Kris. And off they went.

The misty rain became more of a drizzle as they approached the first house.

"Oh dear," said Sarah. "I'm afraid that the greetings and names I put on might wash off in the rain."

"This is worse than the ice pellets that were falling earlier," said Kris.

"Yes, at least they would bounce off of you. This is making quite a mess," she said.

"Try covering them with this old blanket," suggested Kris while stopping the wagon.

Sarah took the blanket, went to the back of the wagon and tucked it in place so that it would cover most of the gifts.

"I covered the presents as best as I could, some of them might still get soaked," she said.

The arrangement of gifts in the wagon was carefully planned so that it matched the route of the trip. As they made their way through the village, the gifts that were on top would be for the children whose homes they passed first. If two houses were nearby, Kris would take a present to one of the houses while Sarah would go to the other house with a gift.

As the night went on, the rain tapered into a mist. But this was enough to be a problem. "Kris, it looks like our messages on the presents are starting to wear off," said Sarah.

"I thought they might, he replied. "But I think the children will figure out which toys belong to them."

"I hope so," replied Sarah.

It didn't appear that anyone was aware of these two very wet people, a wet horse and one very wet dog. "With only one house left, looks like we did it. I don't think anyone has seen us," said Kris.

Sarah nodded her head in agreement, "The rain and mist is a mixed blessing, it helped to keep us hidden but drenched the presents."

The last house was Tommy Bullis' home. "Tommy is the nastiest spoiled child in this town. Not only is he a bully, he uses his family's wealth to tease some of the village's poorer children. I wish I could find something to like about him," said Kris.

"Can you describe how he teases those children?" said Sarah.

"Oh he'll bring a brand-new ball down to the park to show it off. While the other kids are playing with a beat-up old ball, he'll taunt them, telling them how awful it must be to play with that old ball. So the kids try to ignore him and they won't even let him play with them," said Kris.

"Could that be the reason he is the way he is?" asked Sarah.

"Maybe he's that way because of the way the other kids treat him. It could be he's just acting out because he doesn't have many friends," she said.

"Many friends? I doubt he has any friends," said Kris.

"He probably feels left out," said Sarah.

"He bullies them and they bully him right back; it's kind of sad," he said.

"Well, there is his house. Sarah can you reach behind you and get his package?"

Sarah reached back and pulled up a big blob of soggy wrapping paper.

"Oh no! Where are the stockings? I made them especially for Tommy, now I can't find them," she said.

"Did we lose them?" asked Kris. "I'll stop the wagon, I'm sure they are back there somewhere."

"I found them," cried Sarah. "But look at them, they're a mess."

Kris, in an inpatient voice, said, "Let's go, Tommy has enough of everything. I'm sure he doesn't need them."

"Kris!" Sarah said with a stern voice. "We are not leaving until every child gets a Christmas present. Now let me think."

Kris lowered his head, looked over to Sarah and said, "I'm sorry, I will try to remember that every child is important. I would hate to be the only child in town not to get a Christmas present. It might make Tommy feel even more left out."

"We're running out of time. We have to find a way to make this right and sunrise is not far away," said Sarah.

Well it was a mess. Kris, Sarah, and Billy were wet and cold. Sarah knew that somehow she had to figure out a way to deliver a pair of stockings to the meanest, nastiest boy in town. The gift was covered by all the other presents but it was near the wheel where it was being splashed with mud for the entire trip. They couldn't even use the wrapping paper because it was destroyed.

"There is a small stream nearby, I can rinse them out. That should get the mud out," said Kris.

Sarah went looking for something that could be used to dry the stockings, but everything they had was soaked.

"Did you find anything?" said Kris.

"No luck, there's nothing dry that we can use. We just can't leave them on the porch, no one will ever think it was a Christmas present, and might think it's a cruel joke," said Sarah.

Kris stood, hands on his hips, trying to think of an answer to the problem. Every child in the village would be getting a gift on Christmas morning except for one, Tommy. He knew that it would be very cruel to the young boy. Even though Tommy wasn't the nicest child in town, he should still receive a present. But the stockings were soaking *wet and the packaging could not be salvaged. Off to the East, the sky was just beginning to show the first sign of dawn.*

Suddenly, Sarah turned to Kris and said, "Do they still have a pet dog?"

"No, old Sandy died a few months ago," said Kris. I was talking to Mr.Bullis just the other day and he was thinking about getting a Golden retriever puppy like Casey. But he hasn't got one yet."

"I have an idea. Kris, ring out the stockings as much as you can. I think there is a way we can give Tommy his gift. Kris squeezed the stockings as hard as he could, letting the water spill to the ground. Then he whirled them over his head to try to stretch and dry them out.

"What do you have in mind?" he asked Sarah.

She answered, "I know it's risky, but once they had a huge dog. A St. Bernard I believe. That dog was able to get in and out of the house through a pet door. I think I can get into the house that way."

"Then what?" asked Kris.

"Then we'll put the stockings near the fireplace where they can dry."

"You mean we are going to sneak into the house?" he asked.

84

"No, I'm going to sneak into the house. Kris you're too big to go through that little door," she answered.

"Sarah I can't let you go in there, what if they awaken and find you? Then what?"

"And what if they awaken and find you?" she answered.

"I can't let you do this," said Kris.

"It's the only solution. You said yourself, every child should get a Christmas gift," she countered.

"I'm against this, this is not part of the deal," he replied.

"Let's find out if that pet door is still there," said Sarah.

Kris shook his head, shrugged his shoulders, and muttered something.

They quietly went to the back of house where they did find the pet door. Kris knew that he could not fit through the small door but Sarah easily could. Reluctantly he said, "Okay, you can go, but please be careful."

"Yes, I'll be careful. I think I remember where the fireplace is," she said.

Kris explained the layout, "The fireplace is just around the corner to the right side. It should be easy to find and it should give you enough light."

Sarah took off her coat, untucked the pillows from her tummy and removed her hat.

"I'm ready," she whispered. "But first I need some stones, a couple of them."

"Why do you need stones?" he asked.

"I need something to hold the stockings on the mantle and I also need something to put in them to stretch them out so they won't get wrinkled."

Kris went to the back of the wagon and quickly returned. "Here, try these. If you must do this, please, please be careful."

Sarah took the objects from Kris and said, "Yes, I will be very careful." Sarah then squeezed through the small door. Moving as quickly and quietly as she could, made her way through what she believed was a kitchen and into the living room. There in front of her was the warm glow of the fireplace. Its warmth radiated to her and made her realize how cold she was. Wasting no time she took the objects Kris had given her and placed them into the stockings. He had not given her enough stones as she thought. Luckily there were some pegs on the mantle that were meant for drying gloves. She hung the stockings and quickly made her way back to the kitchen. She squeezed herself out through the small door.

"We did it," she said in a quiet whisper, as she emerged from the small opening.

Kris helped her get to her feet and said "Thank God you're okay."

"Great job, you did it!" he said.

"You mean we did it," she corrected him.

"Yes, we did it," he answered.

"I'm very happy we decided to do this," said Sarah.

"I'm just glad that you convinced me to do this. I was ready to call it off. I'm very happy, and I hope we made a lot of children happy," he continued.

"I'm sure we did," she said.

Kris and Sarah huddled together trying to keep warm. Billy picked up his pace when he realized they were on their way home. He almost broke into a gallop.

"I've never seen Billy move so fast. His legs are going in all different directions and he looks quite comical," laughed Kris.

"Getting out of these wet clothes can't be soon enough for me," said Sarah.

They were just pulling into the shed when Kris asked, "What did you do with the stockings at Tommy's house?"

She replied, "I just hung them on the fireplace mantle where the fire will help to dry them."

"How did you hang them?" he asked.

"There were some pegs on the fireplace mantle and they were in a perfect spot so they would dry quickly. I put all the stones into the stockings so they would be stretched, and they shouldn't shrink as they dried. I just hope Tommy doesn't think the stones were the present," she laughed. "By the way Kris, where did you find those stones so quickly?"

"I remembered that that there were some left over from our last shipment," he said.

"Our last shipment?" she questioned. "I know they didn't feel like regular stones, and it was too dark to see what they were. So what were they?"

"Just lumps of coal." he answered.

CHAPTER 10

At the end of each chapter the characters slowly retreated back into the page. David would then stand up to read the title of the next chapter and return to his seat:

"CHAPTER FOUR – CHRISTMAS MORNING"

As he turned the page, he was surprised to see that the next page was folded. He took one corner of the page and slowly opened it. The uncurling of the folds revealed the next scene. This time the paper cutouts popped up from the page just as some greeting cards do. And then, just as quickly, they changed into the three-dimensional tableau that continued the story.

The house greeted Sarah and Kris with a pleasant warmth from the glow of the fireplace. They both shed their soaking wet clothing, changed into pajamas, and stood before the fireplace in an attempt to warm up. Kris added more firewood and before long the fire burned brightly, warming them and the room.

Sarah went to the kitchen, warmed up some milk and prepared two cups of hot cocoa. "We need to take a short nap before we go to the church services," said Sarah as she entered the room. "Oh dear, I guess the cocoa will have to wait." Kris was in his easy chair already fast asleep.

"I wish I could fall asleep as easily as you do Kris," she said to herself. Sarah then went to the bedroom, took a blanket from the bed and used it to cover the sleeping Kris. She went back into the bedroom, reached under the bed, and pulled out a package. It was decorated with the same Christmas symbols as the children's gifts were. She placed the package on a small table in front of Kris. "Merry Christmas Kris, I love you," she said quietly. Sarah stretched her arms and laid down on the couch and she too fell asleep.

Sarah was awakened by the sound of paper being torn. When she opened her eyes she saw Kris, sitting on the floor with his legs crossed opening the gift she had set on the table.

"Since we gave all the children in the village a Christmas present to celebrate baby Jesus's birthday, I thought I should give you a present too," said Sarah.

"Sarah, how did you find the time to do this?" he asked.

"Well I must confess, I made this long before we got real busy, just when we started talking about making Christmas presents for the children. I thought that it would be a nice idea for me to give you a Christmas present."

Kris opened the package and found a bright red shirt. He held it up in front of him and said, "This is a beautiful shirt, may I wear it to church?"

"I would be happy if you would," she answered.

Kris put the shirt on, stretched his arms out, and asked, "How did you know my size?" They both laughed and Kris said, "Thank You."

"You are welcome and I must admit you look very handsome, mister! Excuse me now, I must get ready for church, I need to comb my hair," she said.

"Yes we both need to get dressed, it's getting very late and church will start soon."

Sarah began combing her hair. In one hand she held the brush, in the other hand a small mirror. Through the reflection in the mirror she saw Kris standing behind her. He had a somber look on his face that made Sarah think something was amiss.

"Honey," she asked, "is something wrong?"

"Yes, you are very thoughtful. You gave me a Christmas gift, but I did not give you one, and it makes me unhappy."

Sarah turned to him and said, "I didn't give you a gift with the expectation of receiving one in return. Please don't feel bad."

Kris smiled and said, "It's true, I didn't give you a Christmas present. At least not yet!" With that he went to the doorway and picked up a box he had hidden in his workshop. He gave the box to Sarah and said, "Merry Christmas. Be careful it's—fragile."

Sarah opened the box immediately and saw her own reflection. It was a mirror, a mirror that was set in a picture frame, the type that could be hung on the wall. Kris took the mirror from Sarah and said, "I planned ahead, and put this little nail right here," he said as he hung the mirror in front of Sarah.

"Thank you Kris, it's perfect and I won't have to use that silly little mirror again. How on earth did you know it was something I would like to have?"

"Remember, I'm the mailman, I walk every street, enter every store, and talk to a lot of people every day. Let's just say a little bird told me," he answered.

"Did that little bird happen to be the owner of Milly's General store?"

Kris put his arms around Sarah and gave her a big hug and said, "Yes, Milly said that you had been in recently and really seemed interested in it."

"So I thought since you were giving Christmas gifts to the children, I would give you one too."

Sarah looked at Kris's reflection in the mirror and said, "I think we may have started a tradition."

Kris quickly got dressed, combed his hair, and went to the barn to get the carriage ready. The rain had stopped and the sun was beginning to break through the clouds. It looked like it would be a bright sunny Christmas Day.

Old Billy was still asleep when Kris entered the barn. Kris entered the stall and petted his old friend. "I have to wake you up old buddy." Billy stretched his old bones and finally stood up.

"I know Billy," Kris said as he placed a harness on him. "We had a long night, but I promise you a good rubdown when we get back from church." Billy looked back at Kris and perked up his ears as if he understood. Just then Casey barked. "Sorry Casey, you have to stay home, but when we get back from church I have a nice rawhide bone for you. And I'll make sure that you get a nice rubdown too."

Sarah came to the barn, her hair was done up in a bun. "Your hair looks lovely done up in that way, but then you look lovely no matter how you fix your hair," said Kris.

"Thank you, my handsome husband," she replied.

"We have just enough time to get to church. I'm sure there's a ruckus about last night," said Kris.

Sarah climbed onto the carriage and Kris led Old Billy out of the barn. He climbed onto the carriage as Old Billy started moving.

"Yes, I'm eager to see the results of our midnight visit," she said. As they grew nearer, they could hear the church bells ringing. Old Billy was moving as fast as he could. The time had long passed when he could break into a trot.

"Old Billy has been a great part of our family. I hope we can keep him for a long time," said Kris.

"Yes he has been; I don't think we could have gotten along without him," she said.

When they arrived at church, there was a large crowd standing and talking at the entrance. This was very unusual, but it was not surprising to Kris or Sarah.

"It appears that people found the gifts," said Sarah.

"It will be interesting to hear what they are saying," said Kris.

"Very interesting," she stressed.

Some of the ushers in the church were imploring people to enter the church so that services could begin. Pastor Selbert was also calling to the congregation. "People, people it's time for church. I know you're excited about what happened last night but it's time for church."

It took a few minutes but eventually the crowd slowly filed in and took their seats. The sermon

was very different from what a normal Christmas sermon would be. The sermon was naturally about the birth of Christ, but the Christmas gifts and the Christmas greetings were used as examples of Christ's gifts to people. The good Father spoke of the meaning of Christmas and how last night's events meshed. He thought this was an excellent idea of giving gifts and that perhaps this could happen again. Kris and Sarah later found that the sermon in the other church was similar.

As the service ended, the congregation quickly filed out and headed for the town park. Kris and Sarah listened to the chatter of the people as they walked along. Some individuals were wondering who gave these gifts, while others were simply delighted about the whole affair.

As they neared the village square, they could see a large crowd of townspeople gathered near the gazebo. There were several other small groups almost encircling the larger group. "Let's go over there," said Sarah, pointing to the largest group. Standing on the fringe of the crowd they could sense that there was a mix of joy and uncertainty about what happened the previous night.

The village square was a meeting place where people gathered to socialize or whenever there was a special or unusual event. And this was both a special and unusual event. "I can't recall a bigger crowd. There are some people here I've never seen before," said Kris.

"Could they be visiting friends or family?" asked Sarah.

"I guess so," answered Kris.

The crowd was so large that Kris had to stand on his tip toes and jump up and down to see between the people's heads that stood before him. Sarah didn't even bother to see over the shoulders of the group. With her head down, she tried to listen to the speakers and identify them by their voices.

"I saw them. My dog woke me up and I looked out the window and there they were," said Eddie Sawyer. "Yup, there were two of them. The older fellow was kind of plump and had a white beard," he said. Eddie Sawyer was surrounded by a group of parents and children who had gathered next to the gazebo. "I saw them as they passed under the gaslight across the street from my house," he continued. "I thought it was strange for them to be out on such a cold and rainy night, but I wasn't about to ask them who they were or what they were doing, so I went back to bed."

Constable Jeffery was asked by Steve Carlson, "I hear they were inside people's houses, is that true?"

"Well it seems so because there were a pair of stockings hung by the fireplace with pieces of coal in them. But how they got into the house is a mystery. Mrs. Irene and another person said they were rather large folks, too big to get through the opening of the backdoor," he said. "The house was locked tight. There was no way they could get in, all the doors were bolted from the inside," he finished.

"What did he do, come down through the chimney?" someone shouted. The crowd laughed along with Kris and Sarah.

The focus of the crowd quickly changed when Lucy Kaye pointed out, "I noticed that the quality of clothing was excellent, something Maryanne Tierney or Sarah Kringle might make. She then turned, stepped up on her toes looking around the crowd, trying to find either Maryanne or Sarah.

"I thought I saw Sarah here," she said. "There she is." The crowd in front of Sarah parted as a curtain on a stage might. All eyes were on Sarah when Lucy Kaye asked, "Did someone purchase a large quantity of clothing recently Sarah?"

Sarah glanced at Kris and in full honesty said, "No." The crowd's attention quickly shifted back to Constable Jeffery.

"Whew," whispered Sarah. "If she had asked that question in another way, our secret would have been gone."

"You answered truthfully and that is all that matters," replied Kris.

More villagers were gathering. The newcomers asked questions that had been previously asked and the answers repeated for them. The question about Sarah making clothing came up again but Stanley Kress, the village blacksmith, handled it, "We already asked Sarah if she made the clothes and she said no, that's good enough for me."

Kris gave Sarah a little nudge knowing that the original question was, "Did someone buy clothing?" And thank goodness it was not, "Did you make the clothing?" Their secret was still safe.

"They didn't do any harm did they?" asked a parent changing the subject. "It does not appear that their intentions were anything but good," said the Constable. "Why would they do this?" asked another. The pastor of the other church spoke up, "Maybe they are saints or angels or maybe just good people. Perhaps since we can't give baby Jesus a birthday present, we should celebrate His birthday by giving presents to the ones we love." His answer caused the group to pause, and the mood of the crowd changed from apprehension to a feeling of good will.

When the other services were over, the crowds once again gathered. Sarah and Kris walked slowly, listening for clues regarding the moods of the crowds. As they passed a group of boys that were discussing the gifts they had received that morning, Kris couldn't help but overhear one of the boys.

"Tommy got coal in his stocking," the boy laughed, along with all the rest of the group.

"I need to correct them," said Kris.

"No Kris," Sarah said, reaching for his arm. "Let's think this out, before you say something. If you tell them why he got coal in his stocking, they might think you had something to do with it."

"I know you're right Sarah, but we may have just made it worse for Tommy. The boys will tease even more and it will be our fault," he said.

"Let's walk over to them and see if we can change their minds," she said.

"Hi Mr. and Mrs. Kringle," one of the boys said as they drew near.

"Well boys, did you get any Christmas presents?" asked Kris. They all tried to speak at the same time, offering to show the gifts of which Kris and Sarah were well aware.

"Did you hear that Tommy Manner got coal," laughed Aaron Wells.

"Was your gift something better than Tommy's?" asked Sarah.

"You bet! All of ours were," hollered Gary Frost.

"We are going to show them off to make him feel bad," said Mickey Brown.

"You boys don't like Tommy do you?" asked Kris.

"No way," said Jimmy Joseph, "he always teases us."

"So you don't like someone who teases you because he has better stuff than you have," said Sarah.

"If you tease Tommy with your better gifts, you will be exactly like him. You will become exactly what you don't like about him," said Kris.

"I guess you're right Mr. Kringle," said Trevor Hall. "I don't want to be like Tommy. As the boys slowly wandered away, Sarah said, "I think we spoiled their fun, but it was the right thing to do."

"Yes it was," said Kris. "Maybe Tommy will think twice about his actions. We can only hope."

Kris and Sarah walked toward a group of adults that were involved in a rather animated discussion. "What's going on?" asked Kris. Several of the group began talking at once, finally Ed Freeman, the village shoemaker called out, "People, people one at a time please. Mrs. Joseph, please tell us what you know."

"Well it seems that many of the village children found gifts on their front porches this morning, all wrapped up in pretty paper."

"From whom did the presents come from?" asked Jessica Law.

"No one knows, the rain washed the names off. No one has been able to read what was written," said Allison Brown.

"You said only some of the children received gifts," asked Kris, looking and sounding puzzled.

"Yes, almost every child received some sort of a present; the younger ones toys and the older ones clothes," replied Kim Hamlin, a teacher from the village school.

"Which children didn't receive presents?" asked Karen Wilson, the local candle maker.

"I know my son Kolton didn't receive a gift," said Suzy Rowe, the lady who took care of the village elders.

"Whoever these people are, they aren't very nice, giving presents to some children but not to others," said Marianne Brock.

"I won't mention any names, but there's a certain boy in town, and you know who I mean, even he got a gift," said Terry Christie.

"Yes he did, but it was some lumps of coal," laughed Trudy Harelson.

Sarah whispered to Kris, "It seems we may have caused a problem."

"Maybe some families didn't find their packages, and when they do everything will be straightened out," said Kris.

"I hope so," one of the crowd replied.

"Yes I am angry," said Rick Scott, "I was always taught that if you don't have enough for all, just don't give to any."

Someone in the group called out, "Hey Kris, you are the mailman. You know everyone in town. Who is so mean that they would leave presents for some children and ignore others?"

"I don't think there is a person in this town that would do such a thing. Maybe there's been a mistake," said Kris.

"There's no mistake, they had favorites whoever they are," called Sandy Draye.

"Yes, they had their favorites and didn't care about the feelings of the others," a voice from the back of the crowd called.

Just then 13-year-old Alfred Hill came riding in on his bicycle waving a package. "I got one, I got

a Christmas present," he called. "It was on the front porch; I didn't see it this morning. My brother got one too!" Almost immediately all of the children that didn't have presents were pleading with their parents return home. "Mommy, daddy, let's go home quick!" they cried. The parents seemed as eager as the children and they quickly left, leaving Kris and Sarah standing alone.

"Whew," said Kris. Sarah nodded in agreement, knowing that all the children would soon have their presents. "Too bad it happened this way. I never thought that some families would not find their gifts on the porch," he said. "Next time we'll have to leave them in the house," Sarah laughed. Kris rolled his eyes and said, "I'm sure that's going to happen," he said sarcastically.

"Too bad the rain washed the greetings off the presents," said Kris. "I know you spent a lot of time wrapping and writing the greetings."

As they began walking toward the carriage Kris asked Sarah, "What exactly did you write on the gifts? I was so busy I didn't have a chance to really see them."

"We were both busy so I just used your *Special Child* stamp and then added their name," she answered.

A small group of people approached Kris and Sarah. One man held out a piece of wrapping paper and asked Kris, "Do you recognize the handwriting from this package?" "Tell us who is it" asked Ken Stone.

Kris took the paper, examined it, and said, "It's barely legible. It's streaked from the rain with some of the letters barely readable and others completely missing." He returned the paper and said, in complete honesty, "It doesn't look like any kind of writing that I've seen before."

"A little girl named Becky held a piece of wrapping paper and said, "I know who gave us the presents."

Fortunately all eyes were on the little girl. If they had been looking at Mr. and Mrs. Kringle they might have seen a strong reaction. How did this little girl know? Did she see them somehow in the middle of the night?

"Tell us, who is it?" asked Mr. Slone. The little girl held up the paper and said, "It's Santa Claus."

"Who is Santa Claus?" asked another young girl named Jennifer.

"I don't know, but that is the name on the present."

"Let me see that," a man said. He took the paper, stared at it for a few seconds and said, "I don't see anything there. "What else do you see? Janet Brown called.

Another young boy brought his wrapping paper and showed it to the crowd, "I think she's right, look at my paper, it does say Santa Claus."

People in the crowd took turns looking at the paper trying to decipher what it said. They were looking at the 'for a special child' stamp and somehow made it into Santa Claus.

"May I see the writing?" asked Kris. He took the paper, held it up into the light and thought it was impossible to get Santa Claus from what he saw.

"Well," he paused, "in the first word, the first letter looks like an F, and I think there is an O in there."

"From," the young boy said. "From, the first word is from."

"From who?" called Carol Waters? "What's the last name?"

The boy pointed out that the first word was from. Using your imagination you could see the word from instead of the word for.

"The next letter is definitely an S," replied Kris. Of course both Kris and Sarah knew that the next word was the word special. He then showed the wrapping paper to the people nearby, they all agreed, it was an S.

"What else do you see?" Dell Bowen called.

"Not much," said Chuck Nelson, "it is too washed out to read."

"Maybe my paper is easier to read," said little Billy Boller. The people around Kris compared the two pieces of wrapping paper. After much discussion the group decided that the name started with the letter S. By comparing three different wrapping papers, there was the possibility of three different names. Somta, Samta or Santa. Little Becky insisted, "I think his name is Santa."

"Santa, what kind of name is Santa?" someone in the crowd asked.

"What did you say his last name was?" asked Mrs. Diane.

Little Becky said, "Claus, his name is Santa Claus."

After examining the last word, Kris said, "Well we are not sure it's Claus, but the best we can come up ...it might...it could be...Santa Claus, just like little Becky said."

"Let me see that," said Mayor Thomas. The mayor, who was a big man, took the wrapping paper and turned it every which way.

"Harrumph," said the Mayor. "There is no doubt, the person who gave these Christmas presents was Santa Claus."

"Mr. Mayor, who or what is Santa Claus?" asked John Meyer, the village doctor. Everyone in the village knew that Mayor Thomas would have an answer, whether it was right or wrong, he would have an answer.

"Well...um....Santa Claus is a very generous person from a far-off country," he blustered. "He gives presents on Christmas to remind everyone of the Christ child's birthday."

"Why doesn't he show himself so we can thank him?" another person called.

"Well he......he....umm..... ahh yes, it says in the Bible to not call attention to oneself when giving alms, isn't that right Pastor Lattimore?" The pastor was standing at the rear of the crowd, when the Mayor called on him.

"Well there it is nice to know that you have listened to some of my sermons, and yes it can be found in the Bible."

"How did you learn of Santa Claus?" questioned Mr. Cushing.

"Well......ahh," the Mayor stumbled, searching for words, "it was.......ahh..... mentioned to me by a traveler that passed through our town a long time ago.

But enough with the questions, it's Christmas Day. It's time for us to all go home to be with our families. Good day to all and Merry Christmas."

The Mayor's words seemed to convince the crowd about Santa Claus, after all he did use words from the Bible.

But Kris and Sarah knew the real story. "Let's go home Kris," said Sarah. "We've had a very long day."

"And a very interesting day, don't you agree?" replied Kris.

As they neared their carriage, two more families in buggies and three children came racing towards them, exclaiming that they too had found presents. "I guess we can stop worrying about the missing presents," said Sarah.

On the way home Sarah asked Kris, "What do you think about Mayor Thomas's explanation of Santa Claus?"

"I like that, because if no one had a name for this mysterious person or should I say persons, people might continue thinking about who really did deliver the presents."

"And we might become the prime suspects," said Sarah.

Old Billy picked up the pace as they neared their home. "I think Billy's had enough for one day," said Kris.

"Billy has had a really good day; I think he understood what was happening," said Sarah.

Kris extended his hand to Sarah as she stepped down from the carriage and said, "I love you Sarah."

"I love you Santa Claus," said Sarah laughing.

"I guess we are Mr. and Mrs. Claus," said Kris.

CHAPTER 11

David once again rose from his chair and reached to turn the page to the next chapter. But this time he could not get his fingers, or even get his fingernails, in position to move the page at all. He looked up at the crowd and shrugged his shoulders. From the audience someone called out, "Santa's back."

Immediately several of the elves ran to the exits. Meghan walked over to David and said, "Santa has completed his deliveries for the first hour of the 24 hours of Christmas."

"He just left a little while ago," said a surprised David.

"I think you'll see that the magic of Christmas can accomplish what seems to be impossible," she said.

"It's pretty obvious that Santa and his sleigh can really, really fly," he said.

"Also remember that there are not very many people living in this part of the world, it's mostly ocean. When he gets to the Americas, North, Central and South America, he'll have his hands full but he'll manage, he always does. Right now the elves are reloading his sleigh and he'll be off again within minutes."

And within a few minutes, the elves were returning. David waited until the crowd settled down and was ready for him to introduce the next chapter.

This time, when David reached for the page, the next chapter flipped open by itself. The familiar narrator's voice announced:

"CHAPTER FIVE – THE MAIL STARTS ARRIVING"

Life in the village returned to normal within a few days. Cool, crisp winter days were interrupted by cold, icy blasts that brought the frozen rain that stung when it struck bare skin. On days like that Kris would deliver the mail as quickly as possible so that he and Casey could avoid that painful experience.

As spring approached, Kris said to Casey, "The days are getting longer, winter is soon going to be gone and spring will be here." Casey looked up at Kris and barked. "Sometimes I think you understand what I'm saying," said Kris. "Wouldn't that be great if you could?"

The seasons made their usual changes. The cold of winter gave way to spring showers; to the heat of summer and into the color changes of fall. It was on an early fall day that something unexpected happened. Kris was sorting the mail when he came upon something unusual. "Casey, look at this," he said. Kris opened an envelope and began to read it to himself. He was making noises like, "hum..." and "umm." Kris stuffed the letter into his pocket and said, "Come on Casey, we need to show this to Sarah."

"Sarah," he called even before the door was fully opened, "Sarah, I have something you need to see." Sarah walked up to Kris with a puzzled look on her face, "Is something wrong?" she asked.

"I'm not sure," Kris answered. "Take a look at this," he said, handing her an envelope.

With a surprised look on her face she said, "It's addressed to Santa Claus!" She quickly opened the envelope and began reading.

"Dear Mr. Santa Claus,

I really love the scarf you gave me last Christmas. I don't want a present for myself but could you give my mother one, just like it?

Please sir, thank you,

Patsy L."

"I think it's cute," said Sarah. "Well Mr. Claus are you up to another secret adventure?"

"Wait, I thought it was a one-time thing," Kris replied. "It was a lot of work and this time people may be on the lookout for us. I don't think we can do it."

"Let's think about it for a while," she answered, giving Kris a big hug. "Maybe there is a way."

Kris sat down in his big chair, stretched his arms over his head then cupped his hands behind his neck. "You are an incurable optimist," he said pointing his elbows at her. "You can think about it, but that's all we'll do."

Over the next few weeks Kris brought home twelve more letters addressed to Santa. Sarah carefully stored the letters in a small box in which she kept her sewing supplies. One evening, Kris was reading the newspaper. Sarah approached him with her hands hiding something behind her back. "I have something I want to show you," she said. Kris looked up to see Sarah holding a Raggedy Ann doll.

"Is this a hint? You're thinking about that Santa thing aren't you?" he said.

"What do you think I'm showing you," she teased.

"A Christmas gift that you think we're going to give out this year. Sarah," he said in a firm voice, "I thought we agreed to talk about this."

"Well, we are talking about it now, aren't we? You know I just enjoyed that whole experience last year. It just made me feel so good, I'd like to think we can do it again. I know it's a lot of work and I think that you enjoyed it too."

"There is no way we can do it. Oh I know we can probably make the gifts and have them ready for Christmas but there is no chance that we could deliver them without being caught," he said.

"What if we deliver them on another day?" asked Sarah.

"What would be the point? We did this to celebrate Jesus's birthday, any other day wouldn't work."

Kris stood up, put his arms around his wife and said, "We both know that last Christmas was the best Christmas that we ever had. I know we both enjoyed the reactions of the children and I know they will be disappointed if they don't receive presents but.... I wish there was a way, I really do."

Three days later Kris came home early. In his hands he held a stack of letters. He called, "Sarah, I'm home."

Sarah came out of her sewing room and said, "My, you two are home early."

"Look at these letters," he said putting them down on the kitchen table. "Santa Claus has become quite popular."

"Oh my," said Sarah, "these poor children will be so disappointed."

"And that's not all," he said. "Look at these." Sarah took the letters that Kris held out to her.

She read one out loud, "To the Saint of Nicholas?" she questioned.

Kris smiled and shook his head as if to say no we can't do this. "The only thing I can think of is that the children from other villages have heard about last year and couldn't remember the name Santa Claus," Kris said. "Here's another Saint Nicholas."

Sarah laughed and said, "Well I guess one of us is Santa and one of us is Saint Nicholas."

The letters continued to arrive over the next several days, many from nearby villages. They were addressed to various versions of Santa Claus. Most were to Santa, some to Somta Claus, a few for Saint Nicholas, three for Sonta, and one to Father Christmas.

"Father Christmas," said Sarah, "that's a new one." Slowly, Kris began to realize that even if they wanted to, there was no way they could produce as many gifts the letters requested and no way could they deliver them.

"There will not be enough time to deliver the presents in the village and the surrounding towns," Kris said. "It took most of the night to deliver just for our little town. There is no way we can deliver gifts to the surrounding towns. This has gotten way too big for us."

"We could if we split up," suggested Sarah.

"Split up?" said Kris.

"Sure, I can do the village and you can deliver to the other towns," she said.

"It's simply not possible. First of all, we have one Old Billy and one wagon. Honey, I know that you really want to do this and so do I but it will just take too long. Look at the four towns that have sent us mail, just to travel to them all will probably take more than four hours. And that's not counting making the deliveries. It's impossible."

Kris went to Sarah, put his arms around her and said, "As my mom would say, if you don't have enough for all to share, then don't give to anyone. That way you won't make some people feel bad."

"I know," said Sarah. "I just wish there was a way."

"Last year's Christmas gave us so much joy. This year's Christmas is bringing us too much sadness," said Kris. Even though Christmas was months away, the village children were already becoming excited about the prospect of another visit from Santa. This fact made them both even sadder. Each night before bed they would pray for a way to solve the dilemma. It looked like there was no hope until the night of the dream.

CHAPTER 12

David sat back with his arms folded and waited for the story to resume. The page turned and the narrator introduced the next chapter:

"CHAPTER SIX – THE DREAM"

As Christmas approached, the mood of the children in the town of Nicholas was hopeful and expectant. Meanwhile the mood in the Kringle household became increasingly sadder. "I wish we never started this," said Kris. His normally confident nature gave way to a man that Sarah didn't recognize.

Kris was sitting at the table when Sarah came up behind him. She put her hands on his shoulders and pulled them back as if a better posture could raise his spirits. "I wish I could find something to say," she said. But Sarah's mood had also changed, their usual dinnertime conversations were almost absent. What they didn't know was that things were about to change because of the dream.

Dreams are sometimes difficult to describe; many times they don't make sense. Occasionally some dreams seem so real that you think they are real. Well this dream was just that: hard to describe, made no sense, and this one especially seemed very real.

It all began that night, when Sara, Kris, and Casey went to sleep. It would change their lives forever.

Casey looked around and saw Kris and Sarah in a strange place. They were in a large room that seemed to be made of ice, but it wasn't cold like ice.

"Where are we Kris?" asked Sarah.

"I have no idea; this is very different from anything I've ever seen." He walked over to the wall, touched it and said, "It seems to be ice, it melted when I touched it. But it really isn't cold."

Sarah also touched the wall, "This is strange, a room made of warm ice," she said.

Casey went to the wall, sniffed it and found it had no scent. She thought about licking the wall, but the last time she licked something really cold, her tongue got stuck. Very carefully she gave a little lick, then a longer lick, and finally a big long sloppy lick. Yup, it was warm ice!

Casey usually can smell things before she could see them, but not this time. While she was licking the wall, a person appeared out of nowhere.

Sarah saw her first, "Kris, who is that?" she said cautiously.

Casey turned and saw a strange person, a person without a scent. She started barking furiously. "Easy Casey," Kris said. "Who are you?" Kris asked. The person smiled, held her arms open to them and walked, or rather floated towards them.

"Regina Custo Hibernis," she replied.

"Is that your name?" asked Kris.

"It is not my name, it is my title," said the lady.

"If I remember my Latin, I think Regina means Queen," said Sarah.

The lady shook her head in agreement and said, "Yes, you are correct."

"Hibernia, as in something to do with hibernation. Are you the Queen of hibernation?" asked Kris.

The lady smiled, "Not quite. Hibernation is what animals do in the winter."

"So, could you be The Queen of Something?" asked Kris.

"My husband and I are the keepers of winter."

"You control winter?" said Casey.

"No one can control winter, we only try to keep it tame, and it does what it does."
"What shall we call you?" asked Sarah.

"You may call me The Lady of Winter or Regina. I am comfortable with both of them.

Kris leaned over to Sarah and whispered, "I don't think this is real. I think I'm having a dream."

Kris folded his arms and said, "This is a dream isn't it?"

"Yes, it is a dream. It is a very special dream. I realize what you're hearing, seeing, and feeling is hard for you to understand. But this is really happening," said The Lady of Winter.

Kris turned to Sarah and said, "I'm having a dream and I'm pretty sure it's a nightmare."

"Well Kris, I'm having the same dream," she replied.

"All three of you are having the same experience," spoke the Lady of Winter.

"Is Casey having the same dream?" questioned Sarah.

"You may call this a dream, but I think later you will remember this as an experience. Would you agree Casey?" The Lady asked.

It was right then and there that Casey realized she could talk. "Yes, that's right."

"Casey! You can talk," said Sarah.

"Yes, it seems that I can. Now I know that this is a dream," said Casey.

"Remember, this is an experience," said The Lady of Winter. "But we don't have much time and I want to explain why we brought you here."

"Where are we?" asked Casey.

"Good question," said Kris. "Exactly where are we and why are we here?" Kris had quickly gotten over the idea that Casey was able to talk.

"And really, who are you?" asked Sarah. She too was no longer concerned about Casey's newfound skill.

"Hey guys, I can talk."

"Quiet Casey, this is a dream. I want to find out more about this lady," said Sarah.

"But I can talk. Let me ask at least one question please."

"Yes I guess we better let her," said Sarah. "When we wake up. She won't be able to."

"Why did you bring us here?" Casey asked.

"Winter is the least loved of all the seasons. I hope that you can help brighten our season."

"Our season?" asked Sarah.

"Yes, my husband and I have been in charge for a long, long time."

"What are you in charge of?" asked Casey. "And who put you in charge?"

"God." answered The Lady. "We are not in charge of winter, we only hope to keep it from becoming uncontrollable."

"What are you, some kind of an angel?" asked Kris.

"You might say that," she answered.

"So let me see if I understand this, God made you and your husband in charge of winter, and you want us to help both of you? " asked Kris.

"Wait a minute, you and your husband are angels and you expect us to help you?" asked Sarah. "We are just ordinary people."

"Oh, but you do have a special powers! Look at how many children you made happy last Christmas. Both my husband and I have tried for many seasons to make people happy but with little success."

"Well if you would stop sending us so much sleet, ice, and snow pellets, my people would be happier," said Casey.

"Yes, I agree with Casey," said Sarah, "it's not that much fun in the wintertime."

"My husband, Hibernis Regem Custos is misunderstood," replied The Lady of Winter.

"Then my guess is that he's the King," said Sarah.

They were so busy asking questions that they didn't realize that the room had slowly changed. It was now much larger than the room with the icy walls.

"I see you brought them here," a gentle male voice spoke out.

"Who are you?" asked Casey, who was so surprised that she didn't even bark.

"I've been given the task of trying to influence winter. You see winter is a beast that cannot be tamed. I try my best to keep it calm but that is impossible."

"Are you the King of Winter?" asked Kris. The man laughed and responded, "No. My wife likes to call herself the Lady of Winter. I'm just Theodore, trying to guide winter."

"You don't look mean," said Casey.

"Casey!" scolded Sarah, "that was rude."

Theodore laughed, and said, "That's okay Sarah, Casey makes a good point. People don't understand my job. You see," he continued, "many years ago I tried to make winter more tolerable. So I kept the cold air up here in the north. It became colder and colder, and the cold air caused large amounts of ice to build up. After a while there was so much ice, even the summers were cold. Large glaciers were formed and began moving south."

"I've heard of that, I think it was called the Ice Age," said Sarah.

"That's exactly what it was," said Theodore, "there was so much ice it covered up the town where you now live."

"So how do you prevent that from happening now?" asked Kris.

Theodore came out from the shadows. He was a large man with a long silver colored beard. He was dressed warmly, but not in what you would expect an angel to wear.

"I have to send the cold air down, so it doesn't build up and cause another ice age. I try to spread it around to different places, but sometimes it doesn't work. Some people get more than others but these people will get a warmer place in heaven."

"Are you an angel too?" questioned Casey.

Theodore didn't answer. He just turned and walked away and said, "I have to attend to business. Unfortunately, I'm going to make some people unhappy."

Slowly, magically, the room seemed to dissolve into a different room.

"How do you do that?" asked Sarah. The Lady of Winter smiled, "We have to discuss how you can help us," she said.

Sarah put her hands on her hips and said, "I still don't see how we can be of any help. We don't have any special powers."

"Last Christmas you proved that you do have powers. Your powers made many children and their families very happy. We would like for you to do it again, to be Santa Claus again."

Both Sarah and Kris stood shaking their heads, "Impossible, we don't have enough time," said Kris.

Sarah chimed in, "I don't have enough time. I can't possibly sew and knit fast enough to make gifts for half of the children of Nicholas, let alone the children from the nearby towns that asked to be included."

The Lady of Winter smiled and said, "We don't want you to give gifts to half the town's children. We want you to give gifts to all the children in all of the towns."

There was a brief moment of silence, "Let's get out of here, or wake me up," said Kris. "This is a nightmare!" Kris started walking, but stopped and looked around. "Where is the door?" he asked.

"I realized that you two cannot do this all by yourself, so at least let me show you how we can help," said The Lady of Winter. Kris stopped, looked back at The Lady and said, "Well, I suppose I will wake up eventually, so go ahead, how you are going to help?"

In an instant, they were in another large room. This room was filled with woodworking tools and machinery and unusual looking people. "Wow," said Kris. "I'm impressed! You have a lot of equipment that I can only dream of."

"Who or what are these people?" asked Sarah. "I've never seen people with such pointy ears," she whispered to Kris.

Casey sniffed the air, "They have no scent," she said. "This must be a dream, everyone has scent."

"Maybe they're angels too," said Sarah.

The Lady of Winter laughed, "They are called elves, and I suppose you might call them angels."

"Why did you say that we might call them angels?" asked Casey.

"Most people think of angels as being holy and kind, but elves...," her voice trailed off. "They can be cantankerous and have to work at being better people before they can be considered full-fledged angels. Very few of them will ever become angels. Many of them have been apprentices for a long time, and I fear that they will never make it."

Kris apparently was more interested in the machinery because he asked, "Who are these strange little people?" Sarah poked Kris with her elbow and said, "Shhh... I'll tell you later."

Then quickly the scene changed and they were overlooking a large room that was filled with many sewing machines, dressmakers' models, irons, and ironing boards. There were many elves sitting near the machines looking up at them. One of them called up, using his hands to amplify his voice and said, "We would love to work with you." Almost in unison all the elves called out, "We all want to work with you."

This time it was Sarah who sighed, "Will you look at this place. This is wonderful." Both Sarah and Kris were awestruck, standing there with their mouths open. Casey took charge and asked The

Lady of Winter, "So how do you think we can make gifts for all the children?"

Kris regained his senses and asked, "Even with all these great tools, I don't have enough time to make all those toys."

"And all those clothes," chimed in Sarah.

"We have the machinery, the sewing machines and woodworking equipment. The elves are eager to learn from you. You can teach them to make the Christmas gifts. They are quick learners and hard workers," said the Lady.

Suddenly they were back in their own home or at least thought they were. "Thank goodness, the dream is finally over," said Kris. "I wonder what time it is."

Sarah went to the window to see if she could see any sign of the morning light. "We're not home Kris."

"What do you mean?" asked Kris as he walked to the window. He then quickly walked to the door and opened it. Both Casey and Kris ran out to find that Sarah was correct. The neighbor's houses were gone, and instead the area was all ice. "Another part of the dream," said Kris shaking his head.

The Lady of Winter suddenly appeared, "Don't you approve?" she asked.

"Approve of what?" asked Sarah.

"Approve of your house, your cabin, I think it is a perfect replica," she answered.

"What are you saying?" asked Kris.

"Well I thought that I would try to make it as comfortable as possible for you while you are here," she said. Kris went back into the house and sat down in his favorite chair. He leaned forward with his elbows on his knees and buried his face in his hands. "This dream is a nightmare, I think it's time to wake up. Sarah, pinch me please."

Once again they were back in the large room that they first found themselves. The Lady of Winter was persistent; "I will wake you up if you would just please consider my idea."

"If we promised to just think about your plan, you'll let us wake up?" asked Kris.

"Kris, we want you to teach the elves how to make toys. Sarah, you will teach the elves how to make clothing. Our plan is to deliver a Christmas gift to each child that wrote a letter to you, Mr. and Mrs. Santa Claus."

"We're not Mr. and Mrs. Santa Claus, we're Mr. and Mrs. Kringle," said Sarah.

"I understand that," said The Lady, "but to those children who wrote the letters, you are Mr. and Mrs. Santa Claus."

"If you let us wake up, I'll consider it," said Kris.

The Lady of Winter smiled and said, "The elves are very quick at learning. I told them that if they behave they will earn a lot of points to becoming a full-fledged angel. Plus, part of their problem is that they have too much time on their hands. You know idle hands are the devil's workshop. With your help we will train the elves to produce toys and to sew clothing. You will make a lot of children happy and help to graduate a new class of angels."

Sarah and Kris looked at each other, "Well, I'll think about it, but what about my regular mailman job?" Kris asked. "How will I be able to do that job when I am here, wherever here is? Just sorting out and then delivering the mail is impossible."

"How did you get here in the first place?" asked The Lady of Winter.

"How silly I am, of course, this is a dream and I remember that you said I could wake up if I agreed to think about it. So I agree to think about it," said Kris.

Casey was lying on the floor in her usual place when she decided to ask Sarah what she thought.

She got up and walked over to Sarah and Kris's bed. She tried to ask her what she thought of the dream. But the only thing she could say was, "Woof."

Kris opened his eyes and said, "Hi Casey. What a crazy dream I had. In it you could talk." Sarah sat up with a start, "What did you say?"

"I said I had a dream where Casey could talk, and some Queen Lady was there," he said.

Casey perked up her ears and tried to speak but try as she might, all she could do was bark.

Kris prepared the coffee pot, and placed it on the burner.

"Did you talk to The Lady of Winter?" asked Sarah.

Kris's eyes grew large, "Yes," was all that he could reply.

"And warm ice" she said.

"How... how did you know?"

"And elves...."

"And the castle...."

Kris's expression changed from astonished to amused. "Ha ha... good try, I must've been talking in my sleep, you had me there for a while."

"No Kris no, I had the same dream. I really did. I want to help the elves become angels." Sarah stopped talking and looked at the expression on Kris's face.

"Wait a minute..., this is one of your best tricks. You are trying to make me believe that we had the same dream. But that's impossible, two people do not have the same dream at the same time," said Kris.

"In the dream, The Lady, said that this was an experience that we all were having," said Sarah.

A confused Kris asked, "What are we talking about?"

"We're talking about having the same dream," said Sarah.

"Like I said, two people cannot have the same dream at the same time," he answered.

"Yes, I'll prove it to you, ask me a question. If I answer it correctly that should be proof that I had the same dream as you," said Sarah.

"What was the man's name, and what did he look like?"

"His name was Theodore and he had a long gray beard."

"Wow, you're absolutely right, but one more test."

Kris called Casey. Casey came to Kris as she normally would. "Well Casey girl, if you had the same dream as we did, bark three times and lift one paw. Casey barked three times and lifted one paw.

Sarah and Kris burst into laughter. "I told you, we all had the same dream," said Sarah. "I wonder, is this another part of the dream? This feels real, just like the dream" said Kris.

Both Kris and Sarah rushed to door and looked outside. "I think we're awake and we are really at home," said Sarah.

"My dream was just so real," Kris said. "Whatever it was, I only wish it were true."

Kris filled Sarah's coffee cup and did the same for his. "What if this dream was not a dream?" asked Kris.

"It's difficult to think anything like this could really happen," said Sarah. "The Lady of Winter said that we should think about it. I know I won't be thinking of anything else."

Kris agreed by shaking his head, "I need to get to work, we'll talk about this later."

Kris was very quiet during the day; obviously his mind was on the dream. When he arrived home earlier than usual, Sarah was waiting at the door. "I'm so glad you are home early. I've not been able to accomplish anything all day," she said.

"I know Sarah. I've been thinking about the dream all day. What if there really is a King and a Lady of Winter. And what if what she said was really true?"

They hugged and in a soft tone she said, "I pray that this is true."

"Me too," he replied.

No one fell asleep easily that evening. They all were wondering if The Lady of Winter would again take them to her castle. Casey couldn't wait to go to sleep, but the idea that she would be able to speak again kept her tossing and turning. Both Kris and Sarah fell asleep before Casey. She recognized their breathing rhythms as they went from awake to asleep.

"Casey, where have you been?" asked Kris. Casey looked around and realized that she too was asleep. They were now all back in the large room that they called the castle. "We were not able to start until we were all here," said Sarah.

The Lady of Winter was happy to see all three members of the Kringle household. "You are here because you want to be here," she said. "If you *didn't want to take part, I could not have brought you here. You always are in control and if one of you decided against coming, none of you would have. It had to be unanimous."*

"Even me?" asked Casey.

"Even you," replied The Lady of Winter. "Shall we get started?" she asked.

"Just a minute," interrupted Kris. "There are a lot of questions that need to be answered."

"I'm sure that you spent most of the day yesterday thinking about what you are undertaking," The Lady of Winter said.

"Most of the day? I don't think I thought of anything else," said Sarah.

"You must have many questions," said The Lady of Winter.

And they did. They all began to speak at once, The Lady of Winter raised her hands as if to ward off their inquiries. "Perhaps I should explain what we have envisioned. That should help to ease your concerns."

The Lady of Winter began to outline the plan. "You'll move here to live," was her first sentence.

"What about the mail?" Kris asked.
"Who will teach the children?" asked Sarah.

"What about our house?" asked Casey.

The Lady of Winter smiled, "I understand your concerns, but if you will allow me to continue," she said in an understanding tone. "I will answer your questions."

The large room dissolved into their cabin away from home. "You will move here to live for a few months prior to Christmas, and after Christmas you'll probably need to rest. Perhaps a vacation in a warm place? Birds often fly south for a few months. You could become snowbirds. Or you could simply return to your real home."

"What about our jobs?" persisted Sarah.

"You Kris, have given many years to the post office and you could give many more. Your young apprentice Sandra is capable, willing and eager to take your position," said The Lady of Winter.

Sarah interrupted, "Kris, you've spoken recently about letting Sandra take a larger role at the post office. You yourself said she would do a wonderful job."

"Yes but Sarah's work at the school, replacing her won't be easy," said Kris.

Both Kris and Sarah realized that it would be difficult for them to leave Nicholas. The children would not have Sarah for their teacher and finding a replacement this far into the school year might be impossible. Kris knew that Sarah would never leave her students in that manner.

"As much as we love the idea of being able to make Christmas presents for the children, we have too much to give up. I'm sure that the town could get along without me, but it could not without Sarah."

"The town of Nicholas will not be without you three. You see, you can be here every day, just like you are here now," said The Lady of Winter.

"Whoa, hold on, you're saying that we can be here in our sleep?" asked Kris.

"We have to have our sleep. How would we be able to function during the day?" added Sarah.

"How did you feel the morning after your first dream?" asked The Lady of Winter.

Almost in unison both Kris and Sarah said, "I felt wonderful."

All three of the dreamers realized that they felt energized the next day.

"So we can stay in Nicholas and our day's activities can remain the same. And then we will come back here in our sleep?" asked Kris.

"Yes, you will be able to do everything, keep your normal activities, and under your direction, the elves will make the Christmas presents. You will find that your energy level will be the best you have ever experienced."

Kris, Sarah, and Casey huddled together trying to make sense of what The Lady of Winter was saying.

"This is a dream. How are we to know that we really can do this?" asked Sarah.

"Since this is a dream, what do we have to lose? The Lady of Winter said that we have to want to come here. She can't bring us here against our will," said Kris.

Casey piped in, "I love this! I can talk here and I want to come here and help make Christmas presents."

Sarah laughed, "This is funny. We're talking to Casey and she is answering us back. I love the fact that you can talk, girl. I think we should hear more from The Lady of Winter."

As The Lady of Winter explained her ideas, there were less and less questions. The plan was for Kris to teach the elves toy making and Sarah do the same for clothing. The Lady of Winter assured them that the elves were very industrious and that there would be plenty of time to have everything done by Christmas Eve.

Both Kris and Sarah would be able to make gifts too, and not just be supervisors. Both of them seemed agreeable to this idea.

The Lady of Winter asked Kris to forward any mail addressed to Santa Claus, St. Nicholas, or Father Christmas to a place called The North Pole.

"Okay so far," said Kris. "How do we deliver the presents?" The Lady of Winter put both her hands to her for head and using her fingers, combed back her hair. "We have a great plan that we are working on," she said.

"Oh great," said Kris. "I suppose that's for me to figure out. You said you wanted us to be Santa and Mrs. Claus. That means we have to deliver the gifts on Christmas. Not only in Nicholas but also in the surrounding towns. Exactly how do you suppose we do that?"

"You will fly," said the Lady of Winter.

"Fly?" said Sarah. "Birds and angels fly, and Kris is neither one of those," she laughed.

"You must trust me Kris," said the Lady of Winter. "Only one of you will be needed to deliver the packages. I need a sign of faith from all of you. If you believe, it will happen."

"And if I don't believe?" asked Kris.

"If you don't believe, it cannot happen."

"Everything we've heard from you Lady, is just talk. You have said a lot of things that seem to be impossible. I need to see something more concrete. Some way you can show us you are sincere. We need some sign of faith from you," Kris said.

"Maybe this is just another part of the dream. All of this seems real but we have no proof that it is real," said Sarah.

"You of course know what snow is," said The Lady.

"Of course," replied Kris.

"Can you describe it for me Sarah?" asked The Lady.

"I don't understand why you want me to describe snow, but yes, it's those nasty little pellets of frozen water."

"I'd like to introduce you to a different kind of snow. I doubt you've ever seen it before."

The Lady of Winter raised her right arm, pointed and said "Snow." From that direction a tiny object appeared. It was about the size of a small bird, but it wasn't a bird.

"A fairy," said Sarah. "A real life fairy."

140

"It's a little person with wings," said Kris. "I can't believe this."

"Are fairies angels too?" asked Sarah.

"Sort of," answered The Lady of Winter. "Her name is Snow; she has something I'd like you to see."

Snow held out her tiny closed hands and then threw something into the air. The objects sparkled as they fluttered and floated to the ground. They were like tiny diamonds or swarms of fireflies. "We call these Snow's flakes, they are tiny crystals, and each one is unique."

"Take a closer look. They won't hurt you." Sarah reached out to catch some of the sparkling flakes, "Oh I broke them," she said.

Kris looked intently at Sarah's palm, "I don't see them. All I see are little drops of water."

Snow fluttered over and landed on Sarah's open palm. "Isn't she darling?" gushed Sarah. Snow reached down to one of the small drops of water. As she picked it up it transformed into a tiny crystal. Then the tiny fairy tossed the flake into the air. It floated down and landed on Kris's coat sleeve. Kris held his sleeve up so Sarah could look at it, their noses almost touching as they examined the tiny white object. "It's beautiful," said Kris. "But I'm not sure what it really is."

"I'll explain what you're looking at," said The Lady of Winter. "Snow collects the first tears of a newborn baby and creates a crystal that represents that child. Each one is different; no two can ever be alike. Just as everyone is unique, so are their crystals. The one that you just looked at was yours Kris. It was made at the time of your birth. We call these crystals 'Snowflakes.'

"Every snowflake has six sides or six points. Honesty, generosity, compassion, decency, morality, and humility are represented by those six points. These attributes in a newborn are balanced, just as every snowflake is balanced. During their lives, sometimes these attributes become unbalanced. When this happens, that person's snowflake becomes unbalanced or broken. When these people are able to regain their balance, their snowflakes also are repaired."

"Wait a minute, newborn babies don't have tears," said Kris.

"And now you know why," replied The Lady of Winter. "The crystals have magic and I am sure that we will put that magic to good use this Christmas."

"You asked for a sign, this is my sign," said The Lady of Winter.

Kris and Sarah woke up almost at the same time. They were back in their home, the one with all its own familiar scents. They knew that the dream was over.

"She said that there would be a sign," said Kris.

"Did you understand what she meant by a sign?" asked Sarah.

"No, I have no idea what she meant. I don't know what to do next. Do you think we will have the dream again tonight?"

"I think we need to wait for the sign," said Sarah. "But I still don't know how the sign will help us to make our decision."

Sarah was looking out the window. Kris and Casey were about to leave for the post office when she said, "I think you'd better bundle up, it looks like it might pellet."

Kris reached for his wide brimmed hat, the one that would protect him from those nasty stinging pieces of ice. "I have to talk to Theodore. He has to find a way to time it when it pellets. I will suggest that the middle of the night when people are snug in their warm bed, would be a much better time," he said.

Kris and Casey were about halfway through their deliveries when something floated down from the sky. It was soft and cold and landed on Casey's nose. In a flash it disappeared into a speck of water. "Casey!" Kris cried. "It's Snow's flakes, it's the sign." The flakes increased in number. They turned the trees and bushes into white objects of art. People came out of their houses to view the new phenomenon. Mrs. Joseph called out to Kris from her porch, "Kris, what is happening, what are these things?" Kris laughed, and called back, "Don't worry Mrs. Joseph, they're called snowflakes."

Sarah ran out of the house. She held her arms up in the air, allowing the flakes to land on her face. She laughed when a large one fell on her eyelashes. Off in the distance she could see Kris and Casey getting closer. They ran toward each other so they could share this event. Sarah picked up a handful of Snow's flakes and threw it at Kris. "And so you want to play rough do you?" he asked, throwing some of the flakes back at her. They played as two young children might and they did it with a tremendous amount of joy. "Let's go down to the village square, I want to see how the townsfolk are reacting," said Kris.

They were amazed when they reached the square; grown people were acting like children. People were picking up handful of flakes and making them into balls and throwing them at each other. The balls of flakes were so soft and light that they would easily break when they landed on a person. It seemed like everyone was laughing.

At the nearby hill, some boys and girls as well as adults were sliding down the hill in bushel baskets. Some adults were too large to fit into them comfortably but that didn't seem to stop their enjoyment.

Near the gazebo some children had fashioned the flakes into the form of a person, using a carrot for a nose and two buttons for eyes. A young girl, no more than four years old, laid down on her back and moved her arms and legs back and forth. When she got back up to her feet she called to her parents, "Mommy, daddy, look, I made an angel."

Mayor Thomas who was covered in the tiny white flakes, was laughing and trying to catch his breath at the same time. "Isn't this great? Have you ever heard of or seen this stuff before?"

Kris first looked at Sarah and then back at the mayor and said, "Yes Mr. Mayor, I have heard of snowflakes. It's really wonderful! Don't you agree?" Mayor Thomas nodded his head in agreement and said, "This is the best thing that's ever happened to this town."

Sarah looked at Kris, took his hand and whispered, "We have our sign."

CHAPTER 13

Before David could stand up, Meghan came to him and said, "Let's take an intermission. I know the elves are hungry and so am I. I think you could use a break too."

"Yes, I could use a break. About how long do you think it should be?"

"Let's say, two hours."

"Two hours seems like a long time," David answered.

"Our cafeteria staff needs time to prepare the food for this big crowd. Let's give them thirty minutes."

David stood up and made the announcement. "We are going to take a two hour break. The cafeteria will open in thirty minutes. See you in two hours."

David's leg was feeling much better and he was able to walk to the cafeteria and have a peanut butter and jelly sandwich with a glass of water. He wondered if Christmas magic had anything to do with his ankle. He asked Meghan, "My leg is feeling better, do you think the Christmas magic has anything to do with this?"

Meghan replied, "I'm never surprised by what Christmas magic can do."

David rubbed his scruffy beard and asked, "Is that a yes or a no?"

Meghan smiled and said, "It's one or the other."

"That's a great answer Meghan," he laughed.

The two hours passed quickly. The crowd was near capacity and anxious for the story to resume. As David stood up to make the announcement, the crowd quieted down, the book opened and the characters came to life. The narrator announced the next chapter:

"CHAPTER SEVEN – SNOW'S FLAKES"

The Kringle household was very eager for nightfall that evening. If they had the dream again, Kris and Sarah were prepared to commit to, as Sarah put it, "becoming Santa Claus."

"After seeing Snow's flakes, I have to believe that these dreams we've been having are real," said Sarah.

Kris stood up, walked to the front window and said, "Snow's flakes are starting to melt away. If we have the dream tonight, I hope that The Lady can erase some of my doubts. Right now I have many questions.

Sarah opened the jar of pears that she had preserved earlier that fall and prepared two bowls, each with three halves. She handed a bowl to Kris and said, "Those flakes are so beautiful, I just can't get over how they changed the spirit of the townspeople. Everyone was smiling, laughing, and having a good time. I had a good time too."

Kris had a mouthful of pears but couldn't help to say, "It looks like The Lady is really trying to make winter into something more pleasant."

Sarah took a napkin and wiped the corners of her husband's mouth. "I just have to believe that this is all real," she said.

Sarah and Kris had a difficult time falling asleep that evening. They alternated between joy and uncertainty. It was hard to believe that this was really happening.

Casey was the first one to fall asleep and found herself in the great Hall. But she was alone. "Where is everyone?" she asked.

And as she usually did, The Lady seemed to materialize out of nothing. "Both of your people are not yet asleep. It seems they have a lot on their mind."

"So what do we do now?" asked Casey.

"We wait."

Casey scanned the room and asked, "May I ask a question?"

"Certainly, what's on your mind?"

"Well as you know, I'm a dog. How will I be able to help? I can't build toys or sew."

"Casey, you will be very valuable. Santa has to have someone to help him with the sled and the toys."

"I'm not big enough to pull a heavy sled," she said. "Even Old Billy has trouble pulling a wagon and he's a lot bigger than I am."

Just then Sarah started to slowly appear. At first she was a faint transparent outline and then she became Sarah as she moved from one realm to the other.

"You finally fell asleep I see," said Casey.

"Hello Casey. Good morning or is it good evening Lady?" asked Sarah. "Yes, I was just so excited I couldn't settle down. Where's Kris?"

"He'll be here shortly," offered The Lady, "or at least I think so."

Sarah was so very excited. She started talking so fast that it was difficult to understand her. "I have some ideas for clothes for the boys and girls. I can hardly wait to get started." She started explaining how she was going to teach the elves to sew when Kris started to appear.

When he finally made the transition, he saw that Sarah and Casey were already there. He looked at The Lady, smiled, and said, "I have many questions." And indeed he did. He fired them off, one after another. "What will happen on Christmas Day? How can we deliver all these gifts to the different towns? How will we know what presents to make for which children?"

The Lady remained calm. "She must be an angel," thought Casey.

The Lady replied, "Only you have the answers to your questions."

Kris's eyebrows shot up, his eyes opened wide. "You have brought us here and asked us to make winter more enjoyable. I feel that you expect us to do the impossible," said Kris.

Sarah went to Kris; she could see that he was very upset. "Kris, relax for a minute. Let's find out more about what she has in mind."

The Lady smiled, "You will be able to answer your questions if you believe," she said.

"Believe, believe in what?" he asked.

"Believe that this is all possible," replied The Lady.

"How can I believe that we can deliver the presents on Christmas Eve to all the children that

150

have already written letters? There are more than twice as many children as last year. I would have to learn to fly to accomplish that. We know that's impossible."

"Are you willing to learn to fly?" The Lady asked.

Kris and Sarah looked at each other in astonishment. Casey jumped into the conversation, "Learn to fly? I thought I was going to pull a wagon?"

"Casey, I never said that you would pull the wagon, I said you would help with the wagon."

Kris interrupted, "Casey doesn't have wings and neither do I."

"All of your questions will be answered, I assure you, before you wake tomorrow morning," said The Lady.

They were not at all surprised when they quickly and silently found themselves in what appeared to be a factory. All of them, Kris, Sarah, Casey and The Lady were standing on a balcony that encircled a large area. On the floor of that room were many elves and woodworking machines.

"We saw this room before. I am very impressed with the machinery. Your people, the elves, how can I be sure that they are able to produce the toys? Do they have the skills to complete the task?" asked Kris.

Seeing people on the balcony caught the attention of the elves. "When do we get started? What do we make?" they called out. Sarah noted that there were many lady elves in the group.

The Lady raised her hands and the elves quickly quieted down. "Mr. and Mrs. Kringle and Casey very much appreciate your enthusiasm," she said. She then turned to the three of them and said, "I think you can see that they are very eager; I can assure you that making the toys and clothing will not be a problem."

Once again the room dissolved and a similar room appeared. This time the floor contained many sewing machines. Sarah noticed that there were many male elves sitting next to the sewing machines. She thought to herself, "This is great, both the men and women elves are not pigeonholed into doing what you might call, man's work or women's work."

"It appears that making the toys and the clothing is not the problem," said Kris.

"With all due respect Lady, the problem is still how to deliver all those presents to all those different villages in just one night," added Sarah.

"Come with me," The Lady said. This time they found themselves outside of the castle. It was a beautiful night, but it was very cold.

"Brrr," said Sarah. "We are not dressed to be out here Lady."

The Lady moved her arms in a circle and pointed at them. "Maybe this will help," she said.

Casey looked up to see Kris and Sarah dressed in the costumes Sarah made for last Christmas Eve. Sarah looked at Casey and said, "Casey your hat matches ours."

Once again the scene changed. They were standing in an evergreen forest. Snow's flakes covered the ground. Off in the distance they could see something moving.

"Reindeer, those are reindeer," said The Lady. "They are very quick and very nimble. A team of them could pull the sled and they can cover a lot of ground with their jumping ability."

"Are they a team?" asked Sarah.

"Not exactly," she replied.

"They're wild aren't they?" said Kris.

"Yes," replied the Lady.

"You expect us to catch them, and train them?" asked Sarah.

"I suppose that Christmas magic can't take care of everything. How do you expect us to catch them if they're so fast and nimble," said Kris.

The Lady turned to Casey and said, "This is where you come in Casey. One of our elves has studied them. With your help we can catch them. Eight or nine might be enough. With some of the Christmas magic, taming them will not be a problem."

"Why don't you use magic to catch them?" asked Sarah.

"We don't have an unlimited amount of magic. We just have enough for Christmas," said The Lady.

The Lady then summoned an elf named Ike Kechum . "Ike Kechum has studied the reindeer. He has captured one reindeer and he will explain his plan."

Ike Kechum spoke in the squeaky singsong manner that many elves used. "I have tamed one reindeer. He was easy to attract but hard to catch. They are so fast and they can jump very high. I was lucky to capture this one. I named him Blitzen, which means lightning. This is my friend Johan. He thought of that name because he was so fast."

Ike introduced four other elves including Johan. "Reindeer are very curious. They will investigate anything that is unusual."

Johan stepped forward holding a string of treaded popcorn and said, "We will place these on certain evergreen trees. This should lure them toward the barn." The other elves showed a variety of objects to hang on the trees. Apples, sparkly ribbons, and candles to light the path for the reindeer to follow.

Kris reluctantly agreed to try the plan fully realizing that this was probably the only possible way the Christmas presents could be delivered in one night, Christmas Eve. The reindeer could move much faster than Old Billy, but could they move fast enough?

Kris went to help the elves decorate the trees with various objects that the elves supplied. Sarah spent all the time working on one evergreen tree, making it more a work of art than a lure to capture the reindeer. "Kris," she called. "This is really fun. How do you like my Christmas tree?"
Kris smiled and said, "Sarah, everything you do, you do it in style."

The Lady reappeared when the preparations were complete. The candles illuminated the path. A gentle breeze caused the shiny ribbons to twinkle and shimmer. The Lady said, "This is beautiful. This is what I would like for winter to be, not cold and drab, but warm and shiny."

Casey was puzzled. She asked, "Where do I come in?"

Ike walked up to Casey, knelt down and put his hands on Casey's head. He looked at her straight in the eye and said, "Casey, you are the only one fast enough to keep the reindeer from escaping. Once they get on the path, your job is to keep them going forward and make sure they don't run back out. Are you up to it?"

Casey nodded her head and said, "I sure am."

The Lady, Kris, and Sarah all went to the barn. Kris and Sarah climbed a ladder that led to the hay mow, where the hay for the reindeer would be stored. Naturally, The Lady was already there. They opened the big swinging door and looked out to find where Casey was and if she was having any luck corralling the reindeer.

Sarah saw something on some of the decorated trees. "Look at the top of the trees, there's something there, something fluttering."

The Lady smiled, "I see we have some visitors. Look at the nearest tree, I think you'll find something interesting."

Kris said, "It almost looks like they have wings."

Kris strained his eyes. He cupped his hands to form a tunnel so he could better see what was on the tops of all those trees. "It looks like they're little children," he said. "And they look like they have wings."

Sarah added, "Angels?"

The Lady replied, "Yes, they are Angels."

Both Kris and Sarah became emotional, tears running down their faces. "Why are they here?" asked Sarah.

"Angels are everywhere, we just cannot always see them," The Lady answered.

Kris and Sarah gazed at the sight of the shimmering trees with the Angels perched on top, and it was breathtaking. The moonlight was shining brightly. The Angels wings were translucent and only visible when the light struck in a certain fashion. It took a few minutes before they remembered the reason they were there.

It wasn't long before the reindeer appeared. There were about twenty of them. They moved cautiously, sniffing at the strange objects. Some stopped to eat the popcorn, biting off one kernel from the string at a time. Others took an entire apple while still others tasted the cranberries that were also on strings.

Ike Kechum whispered to Casey, "Ok Casey, it's your turn." Casey crouched down into her best squirrel stalking position and slowly moved to the rear of the group of reindeer. The moonlight plus the flickering candles on the trees made it quite bright. It wasn't long before one of the reindeer spotted her.

Their first instinct was for them to run away. That was the direction Casey and Ike wanted the reindeer to go.

While Casey was chasing them, she was trying to bark but all she could say was, "Run, run." The reindeer soon realized that they were being trapped. Some of them reversed direction and ran straight at Casey. She had to make them stop so she fluffed up her fur to make herself look larger. She bared her teeth and said, "GRRR," which is what she wanted to say in the first place.

Some of the reindeer turned away from the vicious looking animal and ran into the safety of the barn. Casey giggled to herself, "If they only knew."

Suddenly a group of the reindeer turned and ran straight at her. Casey thought to herself, "What do I do now?" The thought of those sharp hooves and mean looking antlers was not a pleasant one. Casey stopped dead in her tracks. She was about to run off to the side when the reindeer leapt into the air, and jumped right over her. "They really can fly," she yelled.

Casey ran straight to the barn and asked, "Did we catch any?"

"You did well Casey," said Sarah, stroking one of the reindeer under his neck and feeding it a carrot.

"We managed to capture nine and Blitzen gives us ten; that should be enough," said Kris. The reindeer calmed down quickly and were not frightened, not even of Casey.

The Lady assured Kris that the magic, however limited would be enough to make the reindeer into an efficient team for that one evening. Their next task was to gather food and water for the reindeer. With the help of a great number of elves, a large supply of plants that the reindeer might eat was brought into the barn.

"Well they don't eat evergreen needles, but it looks like there's plenty of other stuff for them to eat," said Sarah. She began showing the elves which of the gathered food should be kept and which should be discarded.

A few of the elves grumbled about discarding some of the food they had found and transported.

"Oh, here's one we definitely don't want to feed to the reindeer, it's not good for them," she said holding up a sample.

"That's one I found," grumbled an especially grumpy but very likable elf named Ozzie. "Don't throw it out," he said.

Sarah took the sprig and tried to reach a hook over the doorway. "Kris; can you give me a boost so that I can place this on that hook up above me," said Sarah.

Kris hoisted her up and she placed the green plant on the hook. He lowered her slowly and they came face-to-face, "Thank you," she said.

Kris held her for a moment and they kissed. He lowered her to the floor and as she turned, Ozzie looked up at her and said, "What about me?"

She then bent down to Ozzie, gave him a kiss on the forehead and said, "We'll keep it up there where the reindeer can't reach it."

Ozzie blushed and said, "Thank you for the kiss. I don't get too many of those from a pretty lady like yourself."

"You're welcome," she replied. She turned to find the rest of the elves lined up and looking anxiously.

"What about us?" one of them said. Sarah smiled and gave each a kiss.

Kris stood at the end of the line, waiting his turn. "I think you have started something Sarah," he said.

"I know," she laughed. Sarah gave Kris a kiss and hug, "This has been a great dream," she said. "We should be waking up soon."

The Lady appeared and asked, "Is it still possible that you will consider being our Mr. and Mrs. Claus?"

"Yes," said both Kris and Sarah, almost in unison.

"And you Casey?" "Yes, my lady, I will be happy to help where I can."

Kris and Sarah both knelt down, hugged Casey and said, "Thank you."

Casey could feel herself starting to wake. It was in this half sleep half-awake state when she heard Kris ask Sarah, "What was that weed that you hung on the hook?" "It's called mistletoe," she answered.

CHAPTER 14

"CHAPTER EIGHT – THE COMMITMENT"

Kris woke up first. He went to the kitchen and began cooking breakfast for Sarah and himself. Casey soon wandered in, checked her bowl, and found it empty. She looked up at Kris and barked.

"Casey, if you understand what I'm saying, sit down and lift one paw." Casey sat down and lifted one paw.

"We could be famous. A dog that can understand and perform all kinds of tricks. How would you like that?"

Casey looked up at Kris and shook her head to indicate her answer, "Is that a no?" Casey then sat down and held one paw up and nodded her head up and down. "Or would you rather have Sarah and I become Mr. and Mrs. Santa Claus?" Casey lifted both paws and nodded again as if to say yes. "You are a wonderful dog Casey!"

Sarah was standing at the bedroom door looking into the kitchen. "I think Casey wants to become Casey Claus."

"I'm thinking that I want you to be Mrs. Claus, my dear wife."

"I would be very happy to be married to Santa Claus, my dear husband."

It was evident that all three of the Kringle household were convinced that this was in fact happening.

Each evening, they fell asleep and were transported to a magical place. Each trip, they were met by The Lady, many different elves, pixies and angels.

Sarah met with the elves who volunteered to make clothing of all sorts. Sarah, being an expert seamstress, demonstrated the proper technique to make quality attire. At first the elves made many mistakes and became frustrated. Sarah was unruffled, calm and patiently persistent and changed the elves' attitudes. It didn't take long for the elves to produce the clothing. Two women elves and the male elf even became designers that rivaled Sarah. She was very pleased.

Meanwhile, Kris met with the elves that volunteered to produce toys. Many of the elves were not skillful using the machine, but under Kris's tutelage they eagerly studied and became proficient. Elves love toys and were happy to be making them.

Kris challenged the elves to create new toys. The elves thought that was a wonderful idea. And some of their ideas went into production.

Since quality toys were being produced in quantity, Kris had the time and opportunity to investigate just how the team of reindeer would be used. He went to the barn where three elves were completing a harness for the reindeer. "That harness looks beautiful," Kris said. "You fellows are quite skillful in everything you do."

"Thank you, we try" said Ike Kechum.

"We built it for eight reindeer," said another elf named Forest.

"Why eight?" asked Kris.

"Well they are the eight biggest and strongest of the ones we captured," said Ike Kechum.

"Of the two that are left, one of them is a little unusual. Something about his nose is different. Real shiny," said the third elf Stormy. "I named him Rudy," he said.

"Then there's Olive, the other reindeer. She seems real bossy. She picks on poor little Rudy," said Forrest.

"I think he's a little bit younger. I'll bet he'll be able to help in some way, when he grows up," said Ike.

Just then, an elf named Roseanne came out of the barn leading one of the reindeer. "This one I named Comet," she said.

Comet was not happy when the harness was placed around his neck and body. Roseanne calmed Comet and each new addition with her sweet demeanor and a few carrots. One by one the other seven reindeer were placed in the harness and the team settled down.

The next step was to hitch a sleigh to the newly formed team of reindeer. It was no easy task to walk the eight headstrong animals to the sleigh. In fact it was almost impossible. Each reindeer seem to want to go in a different direction.

Roseanne had an idea. Reindeer run in herds and they are usually led by the dominant males and females. "Let's pair Dasher with Cupid and see how this works out," she said. She then took the team and walked them in a large wide circle. Dasher seemed comfortable being in the front of the team while Cupid was content to be in the back.

"Let's try this one here, he looks like he might work well with Dasher," said Kris. After much trial and error, they eventually did find a partner for Dasher. Cherub seemed like she would be a good match for Dasher. So they renamed her Dancer. A few more trials and they found that some pairs of reindeer worked better than others.

"Whew, that took a lot of time and work," said Kris.

"Yes it did. I don't think that we can finish this today. These reindeer are wild animals. I think they need some rest and so do we," said Roseanne.

"I agree, said Kris. "Let's finish this tomorrow," he said.

The next evening, under a full moon and a beautiful Aurora Borealis, the elves and Kris hitched their newly formed team to a sleigh. Kris climbed on the sleigh, took the reins, and gave them a gentle shake. The reindeer took off running much faster than Kris was prepared for. The reindeer were out-of-control. This caused the sleigh to careen from side to side as the reindeer constantly changed direction, the way they would if trying to elude a pack of wolves.

Kris had to release the reins so he could grab onto the rails of the cart to hold on so he would not be thrown off. The elves looked on in helpless amazement. But thrown off he was, landing in a snow drift that cushioned his fall. When the elves reached him, his head was just starting to emerge from the snow. "Where did they go," he asked.

"Are you hurt?" asked Roseanne.

"No, just my pride is injured."

"Where did they go," Kris asked again.

"They're still running," said Ike.

"This is not good. We have to have them back," said Kris.

"They like carrots. They like the food we feed them. I think they will come back," said Roseanne.

"I hope you're right. Otherwise we will not be able to deliver the Christmas presents," said Kris.

The next day the reindeer returned. They came back as a team with Dasher and Dancer leading the way. Kris and the elves experimented on how to train the reindeer. Kris went to each reindeer and called them by name so that they would become familiar with his voice. They found out that the reindeer responded to a whistle as well as their names.

The elves created another harness that held only two reindeer. By teaming up each pair Kris found it was easier to control them. Slowly, they teamed four reindeer, then six, and then the entire team of eight. It went much better and after a few trials, Kris was hopeful that it could work.

Within a week, Kris was able to drive the sleigh by calling their names and using whistles to direct them. They moved much quicker than Old Billy but Kris was not convinced that they would be fast enough to deliver all the presents to all the villages.

Meanwhile, Sarah was delighted with the effort of the elves. They were quick eager learners. One of the female elves and her boyfriend were surprisingly creative. On their own they created clothing for both boys and girls that was absolutely stunning. Sarah was amazed and she learned something from them.

While Kris was working with the reindeer, things bogged down in the toy department. Rumors were circulating that they would not be able to meet the demand for toys. Sarah caught wind of the problem and went to that area to see if she could help.

She met with Handy Randy and asked him what the problem was.

"They're making all the same stuff. I think we need more variety," he said.

"Well I apologize for my husband Kris. But I know he'll be back with you in a few days. Unless we can deliver the toys, there's no sense making any."

Handy Randy rolled his eyes and started to walk away.

"Wait! Do you have any ideas how we can get this going again?"

"Sure, but no one wants to listen to me."

"Why not? What are you telling them?"

"I'm telling them to make different stuff but they're not listening."

"Do they know how to make different stuff?"

"No."

"Do you know how to make different stuff?"

"Yes."

"Can you tell me how to make different kinds of stuff?"

"Yes."

"Well then please show me how to make something different."

Handy Randy showed Sarah how to make a pull toy that looked like a dog that made a barking sound as it was being pulled. With Handy Randy's directions, Sarah cut out and assembled the parts necessary to make the toy. A group of elves came over to watch her as she constructed the toy.

"We want to make those too," called out one of the elves.

"Handy Randy showed me how to do it," said Sarah.

"When he shows us things, he yells at us and we don't like it."

Sarah took Handy Randy aside and told him what she just heard.

"You are very important to this project, and I know that you can do better. Please try to be more understanding with your fellow elves. You have a great skill that others may not have. I want you to teach me and the others how to make this toy and any other toys that you are thinking about. Are you willing to do that?"

"Sure."

Sarah called a meeting of all the elves working in the toy department. Handy Randy thanked Sarah for giving him the opportunity. He responded in a positive way and patiently taught the elves. As a result, they went eagerly back to work.

Christmas was quickly approaching. During the day Kris and Sarah continued their daily activities in Nicholas. Yet doubts still lingered. Their dreams took them far away to where the gifts were being created and the reindeer were being trained. The hesitation remained: how would the reindeer and gifts be able to travel long, long distance?

They were about to find out.

CHAPTER 15

"CHAPTER NINE – ONE DAY LEFT"

Christmas was fast approaching. Kris worried about how the reindeer would get to the village of Nicholas. He literally did not know where in the world they were. The only contact with them was in a dream. Were they supposed to get there by themselves or was he responsible for their journey?

He was even more anxious about how he was going to conceal a team of eight reindeer from the people of the village. After all, no one in his town had ever seen a reindeer. It would be a shock for them to see these animals appearing seemingly out of nowhere.

"Sarah, we have to talk to The Lady. She got us into this and we have no idea how we're going to accomplish everything she expects us to do. The reindeer, the sleigh, and all the gifts are someplace far, far away from here. How are we going to transport all those things here? She asked us to trust her, and we have, but I don't see how it's going to be done. I'm not even sure this is real, we apparently travel there in our dreams, but maybe that's all this is, a dream."

"Kris, I'm going to trust her. After all she did show us a sign with Snow's flakes. Tonight, let's call on her and ask her to show us how we're going to get the reindeer here."

"Christmas Eve is almost here. It may be already too late to get the reindeer here in time. We really don't know how far away they are. I have the feeling they are quite a distance away. They may be so far it may take weeks, not just days to get them here. If that's the case, then all of the work we've done will be for naught."

That evening, Kris and Sarah once again experienced the dream. They called out for a conference with The Lady. Once again they were transported to the castle where The Lady was waiting.

"I understand that you both are concerned about transporting the gifts and the reindeer to your village."

"Yes, I don't know where we are now, I don't know if we're close or miles and miles away from Nicholas," Kris said.

Sarah added, "We only have a few days until Christmas. There are so many Christmas presents that have to be moved. We have no idea how that can happen."

"I know you've heard this before, on Christmas Eve, at the stroke of midnight, the Christmas magic will be here. Things that are seemingly impossible will become possible. You will be able to travel faster than you can imagine. The power of Christmas magic will allow you to deliver the gifts at an incredible rate. All I ask you to do is what you have been doing; creating the Christmas presents and training the reindeer. Everything else will take care of itself."

Slowly, The Lady began to disappear and they were transported to the familiar surroundings of what Kris called The Elves village. He was still very skeptical while Sarah had faith.

"Kris, you need to trust a little bit more. Everything she's said so far has turned out to be true. I think everything will be fine."

"I hope you're right, I know you've put in a lot of effort. It would be terribly disappointing if this whole thing was just a hallucination."

"Oh my!" Sarah exclaimed. So many things had happened so fast that Sarah just now remembered last year they gave Christmas cards to those who did not receive gifts. "Christmas cards! We don't have any. What are we going to do?"

"I don't know, maybe it's too late," Kris said.

"I'm going to see if the elves know anyone who can help us," she said.

Word quickly spread and soon an elf named Ima Rembrandt found Sarah. "I understand you need someone who has artistic ability," Ima said. Sarah was delighted and explained to Ima what they did the previous year. Ima was an artist and she was very interested in helping with the project. Within a few hours she created several different designs.

"These are beautiful Ima, thank you so very much," said Sarah.

"How many of these do you need?"

"That might be a problem. We will probably need over 100."

"Would you like them to all be the same or would you like a variety?"

"A variety would be ideal. Could you do that for us? We need these by tomorrow."

"I have four good friends who can help me. We have a printing press and once I make the etchings, printing the cards will go quickly."

"That would be wonderful, and thank you."

Kris spent the greater part of the day working with the team of reindeer. His verbal commands and whistles seemed to be working very well. They were not perfect but they were getting better each time. On his last trip the reindeer were moving quickly, almost stride for stride in unison. Kris was sure they were moving the fastest they ever had. They were quickly approaching a fallen tree trunk that they usually turned to the left to avoid. Kris gave a whistle and called out for the team to slow down. The team didn't slow down, in fact, they ran directly at the fallen tree. Instead of turning, they leapt into the air as a team, taking Kris and the sleigh high over the log. Kris screamed, "Are you trying to scare me to death?" The team and sleigh effortlessly glided and softly landed.

He called out his command for them to stop and they did. He exited the sleigh and went to each of the reindeer, scratching them behind their ears and talking to them softly. "Maybe I'm wrong, maybe you can fly. We will see tomorrow."

Kris went back to where Sarah was finishing up the odds and ends. One of the things that needed to be done was wrapping the Christmas gifts. "What are we going to do? We don't have any wrapping paper," said Sarah.

Ima was nearby and heard Sarah. "What is wrapping paper?"

"It's paper that has Christmas designs printed on it. We use it to hide the children's Christmas presents."

"Why do you want to hide the presents?"

"Anticipating what is in the package causes excitement. It's just plain fun for both the children and adults."

"Would you be interested in the other four designs that I created for the Christmas cards? We could easily use them in a random fashion to put the on paper."

"Will you have time to do this and have it ready by tomorrow so that we could wrap the presents?"

"Yes, it will be done."

"Oh thank you again Ima. It'll be the icing on the cake."

"Icing on the cake? I don't think the paper will be edible."

Sarah laughed, "No Ima, I just meant it would be the perfect finish for our project."

Kris and Sarah once again called upon The Lady. Within seconds they were transported back to the castle.

"We think we're ready. The reindeer seem ready and the toys and clothing are ready to be wrapped," said Sarah.

"We've done as much as we can do. You said that Christmas magic would help us with the rest," Kris said.

"Theodore and I have been watching you. Like you, the elves and the angels have been preparing for that day as you have. Christmas magic will begin at the stroke of midnight on Christmas Eve.

At that midnight hour, it will be Christmas in one very small part of the world. And one hour later, another small area of the world will welcome Christmas. This will happen a total of 24 times.

But for the village of Nicholas and the other nearby towns that you will be visiting, only once. So sleep well tonight, my friends, because tomorrow will be an exciting and joyful day."

As The Lady slowly vanished, Kris and Sarah slowly emerged from their sleep. "I don't think I will be able to sleep tonight, I'm so excited," said Sarah.

"We better get to sleep tonight, or none of this will happen," Kris said.

The day seemed to drag slowly but finally it was time to go to sleep.

Kris was shaving when he glanced in the mirror and saw Sarah dressed in her almost red outfit wearing a white cotton beard.

"Are you going to sleep in that outfit?" he asked. "Of course, and I think you should too."

"I don't even know if we still have it or where it is."

"Well I do. It was put away in the cedar chest, along with your cotton beard."

"Do you think I should wear it?"

"Look at me. I'm wearing it and you should too."

"I guess you're right. The Lady wants us to repeat what we did last Christmas. I think the outfits are part of it."

Kris finished shaving and went into the bedroom where Sarah had already laid out his red Santa suit, complete with his fake Santa beard. He pulled on the pants that were much too big. Sarah took a pillow and placed it on Kris's belly. Then Kris used a wide black belt with a gold buckle to hold up his pants.

"It's going to be interesting falling asleep wearing this outfit," said Kris.

"Between us wearing these outfits and my excitement, I'm not sure I can fall asleep," she said.

"Sarah, I'm very excited too. Thank you for being so positive. I don't think that I would have done this if it wasn't for you."

"We are a team. We are going to make this happen," she said.

"Every team needs a captain and I think you are the best captain we could have," he said.

They cuddled for a few seconds in their red outfits wearing fake beards. Casey nosed in and then barked.

"I think all three of us are ready for this new adventure," said Kris.

"Good night, my dear husband. I'll see you in a few minutes, I love you."

"I love you back, and good night. I sure hope it's going to be a great night."

Casey barked, wagging her tail to signify that she was ready too.

Then all three of them tossed and turned, but finally fell asleep.

CHAPTER 16

The book did not open to the next chapter as David anticipated. He was unsure of what to do next; should he open the cover, or wait? The crowd grew restless, so he had to do something. He stood up, and was reaching for the cover, when someone called, "Santa's back." Many of the elves again exited the hall for the purpose of replenishing the gifts for Santa sleigh.

Something wasn't sitting right with David. It was about the language the characters were speaking. He called over to Meghan and asked her, "How long ago did this take place?"

"I'm not really sure, only Santa and Sarah know and they're not forthcoming."

"The reason I'm asking, is that the characters are speaking in every day modern English. These events happened many, many years ago. I would think they would speak in the same manner as the people did in their time, perhaps hundreds of years ago. Am I wrong?"

Meghan answered, "No, you're not wrong. This book, along with Santa's Village, have to be kept up to date. The toys that were made many years ago would not be very popular today. So we need to keep up with the times, making sure we are up to date. The characters in the book are speaking so that the people who are listening can understand. Santa appears in many different cultures. He is called by different names in different parts of the world. These cultures are speaking different languages and have different Christmas traditions."

Meghan continued, "If you are French and sitting in the audience, you would hear the characters in the book speaking French in explaining how those French Christmas traditions came to be. For example, Mrs. C has several different names in other cultures."

"Are you saying that this book changes according to the audience? So, an Italian person would hear the story in Italian?"

"That's exactly what I'm saying," she said.

Within a few minutes the elves were returning to their seats. When it appeared that almost everyone had returned and were seated, David once again tried to open the book. But it still would not open. There was unexpected commotion from the crowd. David scanned the room, trying to determine what the disturbance was. A few moments passed when the crowd spotted Santa entering the room. He walked over to where Mrs. C had just been sitting and sat down. He looked over and saw David and waved. David smiled and waved back to Santa.

"Meghan, what's happening?"

"Mrs. C is taking her turn in delivering Christmas presents," she answered.

"You've got to be kidding! I thought Santa delivered all the presents."

"No, she wants to have fun too. So every year, she takes a few trips by herself. She's done that forever. They share. It's really nice the way they work together."

"Don't people notice the difference between them?"

"Very few people ever see Santa or Mrs. Claus in their houses. She wears her almost red outfit along with a fake beard. She looks a little like Santa. I'm sure at least once and probably more than a few times, she's been to your house and you didn't notice any difference."

"Well, I'm sure I've never seen Santa or Mrs. C in my house because I've been asleep when they were there."

I know she's been seen by people when she was delivering Christmas gifts. You know that Santa has a lot of different looks. Some years he grows his beard long and some years his beard is quite short. So seeing a different looking Santa is not unusual. And during the Christmas season, there are a lot of what I call 'Santa's Helpers.' These are people who dress up to look like Santa. So when you think you see a Santa's helper, it could be the real Santa. Santa told me how he's met many people who thought he was a Santa's helper. He loves it. He thinks it's hilarious."

"I can remember an old photograph of me sitting on Santa's lap. Could that have been the real Santa?" asked David.

"Did you feel special when you were sitting on his lap?"

"Yes."

"Then I think you know the answer."

David was about to ask Meghan another question when the book began to open and the narrator started speaking:

"CHAPTER TEN – MAKING PREPARATIONS"

Sarah was the first to awaken into the dream followed shortly by Kris. Casey did not appear for several minutes and was apologetic for sleeping so long. They found themselves in the usual large hall of the castle. The Lady was waiting for them, along with Theodore.

"It's so good for you to come dressed in those clothes. Theodore and I believe you will make winter much more enjoyable. The elves have prepared the gifts, ready to be wrapped. And the reindeer are ready to be hitched to the sleigh. Speaking of the sleigh, the elves have created one that you will be very happy to use today," said The Lady.

Sarah groaned, "This is terrible, it's a mess. Oh no. How could we have done this?"

"What?" Kris asked. "What's wrong, what's going on?"
"The gifts, we don't know who they're going to. That toy, who do we give it to? The letters we

received from the children are back at home. We don't have them here," said Sarah.

The Lady interjected, "If you have the children's letters, would you be able to match them with the gifts?"

"Yes, we would then be able to assign which gift would go to which child," said Kris.

"The problem is, I would have to wake up, get the letters and then try to go back to sleep again? I don't think I can do that," said Sarah.

"I had enough trouble going to sleep last night, and then trying to go back to sleep again?" said Kris.

Theodore interjected, "Is it possible to assign the gifts arbitrarily? Why not just pick a name and assign a gift to that child?"

"We could possibly do that for the children of Nicholas. We know them well enough to match the child with a gift most accurately. But not for the children of the other towns. We don't know what they asked for and we don't know what house, or even village, they live in. We might deliver a baby doll to a household that has no children at all," said Sarah.

"Without those letters, we won't know what children asked for, or even where they live," said Kris.

"The only way we can do it is we have to have those letters. And I don't know how we can get the letters and then bring them back in time for Christmas," said Sarah.

"I can do it, I can fall asleep fast," Casey said, wagging her tail and giving everyone her doggie smile.

"She's right, we all know that Casey can fall asleep easily. You're our only hope Casey," said Kris.

It was their only chance. Sarah gave Casey instructions on where the letters were. But it was a little bit more difficult than just telling her where the letters were, because Casey would have to open a desk drawer and get the letters out. Not an easy task for any dog. But, Casey wasn't just any dog. She would have to fall asleep with the letters in her mouth and hopefully not accidentally or purposefully, chew them up.

"I think we'd better have a second plan in case Casey doesn't make it back in time, "said Kris.

"From memory, I think we could wrap and label many of the gifts for the children of Nicholas," said Sarah.

Kris and Sarah begin the task of matching the Christmas presents with the names of the children who lived in their hometown. Two hours passed with no sign of Casey. "I'm getting worried. Without those letters, we won't know what the children asked for or even where they live," said Kris.

Both Sarah and Kris felt relatively confident about the gifts that would be delivered to Nicholas. Now came the task of assigning left over gifts that would go to the other towns.

"I've separated the gifts into what I think should go to the girls and what should go to the boys. There are a few that could go either way," said Sarah.

"Unless Casey can show up in the next few minutes, I'm afraid we won't be able to deliver those gifts. We don't know which town or even which house they would go to, much less what names go to those houses," said Kris.

"I think we need to tell The Lady that we will not be able to deliver those gifts. I know she'll be disappointed but what else can we do? Maybe she can use some of that Christmas magic to help us," said Sarah.

Kris called for The Lady, but nothing happened. He tried again and still no response. Then, the outline of Casey appeared in front of them. Slowly she materialized and in her mouth was a stack of envelopes. Sarah ran over to Casey, petting her dog as she slowly became awake. "Casey, you did it, you did it!"

"You saved the day!" said Kris.

With the aid of three elves, Kris and Sarah quickly matched names, gifts, and addresses. Four other elves then set about wrapping each of the gifts and attaching name tags.

Finally all the gifts were wrapped and had name tags. "I can match the name tags and the houses in the village of Nicholas. But I have no idea about the other towns. Here's a gift labeled for Patsy L. I know the name of the town and the name of the street, but will I be able to find it in the middle of the night?" asked Kris.

Sarah, her head down, was searching for some kind of solution for this problem. Slowly she looked up and saw the room changing into the room at the castle. And quickly materializing in front of them was The Lady.

"I see you have made all the preparations needed for the trip. And I understand you will be going to places you've not been to before. Please remember that you will not have a problem finding the houses and matching them with the gifts. When you leave on your trip, Christmas magic will be there to guide you. You have nothing to fear. You are about to embark on a great adventure. You will bring joy to those around you and to yourselves. Go forth and deliver your gifts," said The Lady.

Immediately, before they could respond, they were back in Santa's village. "I sincerely hope she's right," said Kris.

"She is right, I'm sure you have nothing to be afraid of," said Sarah.

"I know I have nothing to be afraid of because you're going with me," said Kris.

"No, I can't. There's not enough room for me. Look at all these gifts, I don't think they'll fit in the sleigh now," answered Sarah.

"Or maybe we might have to make more than one trip. Let's load the sleigh and see if you can fit," said Kris.

Kris, Sarah, and several elves carried armfuls of wrapped Christmas gifts to the sleigh.

Kris was the first to see the sleigh and said, "It's beautiful."

Waiting for them was a beautiful new sleigh. It was red with gold trim and was much larger than the sleigh they used for practice. They placed the gifts on a pallet and went to admire the new sleigh.

Kris went to the sleigh and shook it back and forth to test its construction. "It appears to be well made," he said.

Sarah ran her hands over the curves, admiring its design. "It's beautiful. Who built it?"

One of the elves stepped forward and said, "I did, and I hope you like it."

"Who are you?" asked Kris.

"My name is Dee Signer. I installed the white leather seats, super-fast runners, and painted it a beautiful red lacquer."

"You did a wonderful job," said Sarah.

"Thank you, Dee. And now Sarah, you have a seat! Let's finish loading."

Kris decided the gifts and Christmas cards for the village of Nicholas would be delivered first. So the elves began to load the sleigh with the gifts and cards for the outlying towns first. The sleigh began to fill up quickly, and it appeared that the gifts for Nicholas surely would not fit. But as more gifts were placed in the sleigh, somehow the gifts seemed to shrink in size. Unbelievably, the sleigh was able to accommodate all the gifts. It made no logical sense to Kris or Sarah, but Casey said, "I think this is what The Lady was talking about Christmas Magic." The reindeer were hitched, the sleigh was full and Mr. and Mrs. Santa Claus were dressed and ready for the great adventure that was about to begin.

CHAPTER 17

David was amazed at the way the story unfolded. When he was a child, Santa was always there. He never considered the idea that Santa had a beginning. The fact that both Kris and Sarah Kringle were common folks at the beginning astounded him. It appeared that there were only a few chapters left. He sat back and allowed the story to tell itself.

"CHAPTER ELEVEN   –   THE FIRST TRIP"

"Kris climbed onto the sleigh, reached out for Sarah's hand and helped her onto the seat next to him. He looked at her, thinking about how much he loved her and secretly hoping that this undertaking was successful.

In her heart Sarah was praying that this trip would not be a disaster. After all, she was the driving force at the beginning. Now she realized the magnitude of what they were about to undertake.

"Kris, are you sure you want to do this?"

"Sarah, you know that I had my doubts all along, but now I think I'm ready. I hope you are too."

Kris put his arms around Sarah and gave her a hug. They kissed.

"Kris, you know, I love you and I know you love me. That's all we need. If you're ready, so am I. Let's go."

"Now this is the scary part," said Kris. "If there is Christmas magic, it's going to happen when the reindeer start moving. Kris shouted, "Here we go!"

With that said, Kris shook the reins and whistled to the team. The reindeer started moving, slowly and disorganized at first, but in a few moments their legs and bodies became more coordinated. Within a few seconds they were completely synchronized. Their bounds quickly became longer and longer until the reindeer, the sleigh, and the two occupants were flying through the air.

Sarah, with an incredulous look on her face said, "Oh my Lord, we're flying, we're flying!"

Kris let out a yell, "This is fantastic, look how high we are!"

Almost immediately, Kris realized that he didn't know what to do next.

"Sarah, I don't know how to steer the reindeer to where we want to go. I don't even know where we want to go."

Sarah was looking over the side of the sleigh at the ground below and realized they were moving very fast. "Kris, where ever we are going, we will be there very soon."

As they flew overhead, the ground below was covered in almost complete darkness. This quickly changed into widely spaced speckled areas of lights that were probably villages below. The couple had no idea of where they were. They soon felt the sleigh slowing. The straight line arrangement of the reindeer was now spiraling downward.

"Sarah, I think we're coming to Nicholas. Look over there. Isn't that the Village Park?"

"I think you're right. Over there is the church and I think that's the blacksmith shop." The reindeer and the sleigh continued descending in a circular pattern.

"Looks like we're going to land close to the Randel's house," said Sarah.

"I don't think we're going to land close to the Randel's house. I think we're going to land on the roof of the Randel's house!" said Kris.

And land they did on the roof of the snow-covered house.

"What are we supposed to do now?" Sarah asked.

"Do you think I should jump off the roof with the presents?"

"Kris, you can get hurt doing that."

"Maybe we should just throw the gifts over the side and go to the next house?"

"We are not going to throw these gifts into the snow below. They might not find them until spring," she said.

"We could drop them into the chimney and hope that they don't get burned up," said Kris.

"Well, we just can't leave them here on the roof," said Sarah.

"Something is very different here. This roof looks bigger than I think it should be. The chimney's also much larger than it should be," said Kris.

Kris hopped off the sleigh and carefully walked toward the chimney. Sarah called to Kris and said," Kris, you're getting smaller!"

Kris called back to Sarah and said, "No, I'm not getting smaller. The chimney is getting larger." Sarah got off the sleigh and carefully started walking towards Kris. She also noticed that the chimney seemed to be getting larger.

"Either the chimney is larger or we're smaller," said Kris.

"We are smaller, so is the sleigh and so are the reindeer," Kris added.

"It has to be part of the Christmas magic that The Lady told us about," said Sarah.

"Do you think we're small enough to use the chimney to get into the house?" asked Kris.

"I don't think that's a very good idea," said Sarah.

Kris walked back to the sleigh and noticed something strange. One of the gifts was glowing. He picked it up and showed it to Sarah. "This one is glowing."

"It's the ribbon. The ribbon is glowing. Whose name is on the tag?" asked Sarah.

Kris used the light of the glowing ribbon to read the name. "Joanie, Joanie Randel. This must be part of the Christmas magic. We're at the Randel house and the correct gift starts to glow. If only we knew how to get the package into the house."

Sarah was looking at Kris. In the background was the sleigh and the reindeer. "Kris, look behind you. Something is shimmering."

Kris looked over his shoulder and saw that the reins were sparkling. "Well this is it, the reins are telling us how to deliver the gifts get to the house. I'll wrap the reins around the chimney and throw them over the side of the house. Then I'll just climb down and leave the package on the porch."

"I'm not sure I like the idea of leaving them on the porch," said Sarah.

"We can't leave them here on the roof," replied Kris. "If you can think of a better way, let me know."

Kris took the reins. As he began walking towards the chimney, the reins became brighter. When he wrapped them around the chimney the illumination became very intense. "This must be the way," he said.

When he tossed the reins over the side of the house, everything except the part that was wrapped around the chimney grew very dim.

"I think it wants us to use the chimney," said Sarah.

Kris pulled up the reins and then lowered them into the chimney. They became very bright, especially the section that was in the chimney.

"Yes Sarah, the reins do want us to use the chimney."
"But Kris, there is a fire down there. I'm not sure that this is going to work. You could get burned."

Kris looked down into the chimney and then began pulling the reins up. He touched the lowest portion, the part that would have been in the flames. "It's cold. The part that was in the fire is not even warm. Somehow it's been protected from the heat. I have to think that maybe I will be protected too."

"You have to promise me that if there's any sign of trouble you will come back out," she said.

"Okay. Sure, I'll do that."

"Let me hear you say it."

"I promise. If there's any sign of trouble I will come back out."

As Kris climbed up onto the chimney, he seemed to get smaller. "Sarah I am getting smaller? The reins seem very large to me now. When I get to the bottom, toss me the present and I'll catch it."

"Please be careful. I'm scared, I don't like this. This is too dangerous," she said.

Kris leaned over to take another look into the chimney and disappeared!

Sarah ran to the chimney to see if she could see Kris but the smoke pushed her away. She became even more frightened and called down to Kris, "Kris, Kris can you hear me?"

Suddenly, Kris appeared. He was smiling and standing next to the chimney.

He startled Sarah. She regained her composure and asked, "Are you all right?"

"Yes, I'm fine. It was great."

"Tell me, what happened?"

"When I first looked down into the chimney, some of the smoke got into my eye and it teared up. I used my finger to wipe away the tear. The next thing I knew I was standing in the house and standing on the hearth. Then I got concerned. How was I going to get back up? I tried rubbing my eye again but that didn't do a thing. Then I remembered that when I wiped away the tear, I stroked the side of my nose. I tried that but that didn't work. Finally I stroked the side of my nose in an upward direction. It worked! It was exhilarating."

"Do you want to try to deliver the gifts that way?" asked Sarah.

"Sure. Hand me the package and I'll be right back."

Kris stepped to the side of the chimney, put his finger on the side of his nose and disappeared. Within a few seconds he reappeared.

"That was great. It absolutely was fantastic," he said. "I think you should try it, it's fun."

Sarah was not exactly sure this was going to be fun. She hesitantly walked up to the chimney and said, "I'm shrinking so here I go." Sarah placed her finger aside of her nose and brushed it downward. She disappeared into the chimney. A few seconds later she reappeared, laughing. "That was thrilling. I want to do it again." Then she again disappeared and quickly reappeared. She disappeared and reappeared twice more, until Kris put his hands around her body, preventing her from disappearing again. "That is the most fun I've had in a long time," she said.

"We have a lot of packages to deliver and lots of fun to be had," said Kris.

And so it was, the reindeer knew where the houses were, the packages glowed when they were at their destinations, and Mr. and Mrs. Claus had the time of their lives.

THE END

Mr. and Mrs. Claus, the reindeer, the sleigh, the rooftop, and the chimney slowly retracted back into the drawing of the last chapter's page.

The crowd came to its feet as a spotlight shone upon Mr. and Mrs. Santa Claus and their alter egos, Kris and Sarah Kringle. They waved to the audience, acknowledging the standing ovation.

The spotlight then moved to shine on David Carson. David bowed, placed both of his hands on his heart and then pointed both hands back to the couple.

The applause died down and the crowd began to disperse. Meghan came over to David and congratulated him. "You did a wonderful job," she said.

"It was kind of easy, "he said. "The book read itself, all I had to do was get started. The story was fantastic. If people knew the story and how great those two people are, there would be more admiration and appreciation."

"Maybe you might be able to help us with that," said Meghan.

"What do you mean, I might be able to help?" he said.

"I think you know that Santa, Mrs. Claus, the elves and the reindeer are real. Maybe you can think of some way share what you've seen here. If you can all of us here would be grateful," said Meghan.
David shrugged his shoulders and said," Okay, I'll think about it. So, Santa is done for this year?"

"No, not quite. He has many more deliveries to make. This is going to be a very busy couple of hours."
"Well, with both of them are sitting there, I thought they were all done."

"Right now, Christmas is just starting over the Atlantic Ocean. There are very few islands in this part of the world. Greenland has a few small villages. So the population is small and delivering Christmas gifts is quick. But it will soon be Christmas in the Americas. There are a great number of children who are waiting for Santa Claus there," said Meghan.

"Oh I see, they take a short break and then it's back to work," said David. "There are a lot of people living in that part of the world. They'll be very busy."

Just then, an elf came up to Meghan and handed her a clothes hanger with a red Santa suit on it. "This is for you," she said.

"Oh, a souvenir, that's great. Thank you," David said.

"It's not a souvenir, it's for you to put on," said Meghan.

"Put this on? Why?" he asked.

"If you're going to ride with Santa, you have to look like Santa," said Meghan.

David had a surprised look on his face. Could Meghan be suggesting he could ride with Santa Claus?

CHAPTER 18

David was caught off guard by Meghan's comment. "If I heard you right, you're saying if I put on this Santa suit I could ride with Santa while he's delivering Christmas packages?"

"Yes, Santa has invited you to ride along."

"Ride along with Santa? Is that possible? I've never heard of anyone riding with Santa."

"Well, you have a choice. You could ride with him or you could stay here with me. But this is a great opportunity; not many others have been given the choice. So, do you want to ride with him, or would you rather stay with me?"

"Yes, of course, it would be an honor to ride with Santa, but I can't believe that others have made this trip. Who were these people?"

"Well, there weren't that many, but I can name a few. There was a scientist fellow named Albert. He was working on a theory about space and time. He realized that Santa could not possibly deliver all the gifts in that short period of time. So he reasoned that Santa's time was different than everyone else's. His trip with Santa helped him finish his theory.

And then there was a poet who surprised Santa while he was delivering presents to this man's house. Of course, you've heard of the 'miniature sleigh, and eight tiny reindeer' part of his poem. There are a few others that had an influence on world history, but you probably would not recognize their names."

"I don't think I belong to that group, these are very important and famous people. That's just not me," said David.

"You will be the first to travel from here, the North Pole. The others, Santa picked up at their homes," said Meghan.

"Then this is a real honor, I hope I can live up to it," he replied.

"Mrs. C and Santa both think you belong, and they would be disappointed if you chose not to."

"I certainly would not want to disappoint them. I'll get changed right now."

Within a few minutes, David changed into a Santa Claus outfit. Waiting for him was Mrs. C and Meghan. "Well, don't we make a handsome Santa Claus," said Mrs. C.

David then did his fashion model imitation, posing and turning as a model would. "Well, it's a little big on me, but with a few pillows, I'll be just fine," said David.

"I don't think you really need the pillows. Santa himself doesn't need them and doesn't use them anymore," said Mrs. C.

Meghan came up to David and handed him a fake beard, "Try this one."

David adjusted the beard, but it covered up much of his whole face. Mrs. C went behind him and tried to adjust the beard so David could at least see. "Meghan, I think David needs one of Santa's short beards. I think it will fit him much better."

"I'll be right back with it Mrs. C," said Meghan.

"Santa's short beard? I don't think I've seen him in anything other than a full beard," said David.

"Well, just as soon as this trip is over, Santa is going to shave his beard off," said Mrs. C.

"Shave his beard off, why would he want to do that?" asked David.

"We've had a very, very busy season. And after we finish reading all the letters, making all the presents, wrapping, them and delivering them, we take a vacation."

"Yes, but he's Santa, and Santa has to have a beard," replied David.

"Santa and I need to get away for awhile. If he appeared in public in his full beard, people would be coming up to him all the time. We just want to have a little time to ourselves."

"I don't want to be nosy, but where do you go?" asked David.

"Have you ever heard of the expression, snowbirds?"

"Yes, many retired people travel to warmer areas during the winter. I think it's a good idea that you two go someplace warm for awhile. I'm sure it's a good thing for both of you."

"Yes, for a few months, we just want to be ordinary people."

"So I guess Santa needs to regrow his beard each year. How long does it take him?"

"Well, it depends on what kind of beard he plans on growing. Sometimes he likes it short but most of the time he grows a full beard. A couple of times he shaved his beard off, kept it off and wore a fake beard. It was funny when he was mingling with people. They thought he really wasn't Santa Claus. They dismissed him as a Santa's Helper. He's done that more than a few times."

"Wow, so you mean that when I look at someone dressed up like Santa Claus and that person is wearing a fake beard, it might really be Santa Claus?"

"Yes, I'm sure you've seen Santa Claus with a beard and with a fake beard sometime in your life. Most people have probably seen him both ways."

Meghan returned with the shorter beard. David tried it on. It seemed to fit very well with just a few minor adjustments.

Santa entered the room and looked at David and laughed his hearty laugh. "You'll make a fine Santa," he said.

"Not as good of a Santa as you are, Santa," said David.

"I'm sure you're going to make a great Santa," said Santa.

"I'm excited! I'm a little scared but I'm ready and willing to go. I've jumped out of airplanes into enemy territory but this is on a scale that I can't measure."

The elves had just finished packing the sleigh and one of them called out, "All set Santa, ready to roll."

"Let's get going, Christmas is waiting for us," said Santa.

Santa climbed aboard the sleigh, extended his hand to David and pulled him up. There was plenty of room for both of them. Santa jiggled the reins and the reindeer began short jumps in complete unison. Each of their strides grew longer and longer until they began soaring. Even though they were in the air, they kept on striding. Each stride became longer and faster. They were moving at a very fast rate and David expected a very windy ride. But there was not even a gentle breeze. It was warm, comfortable, and very quiet as they were streaking through the air.

Santa noticed that David was tense and gripping the rail with both hands. "I believe you can relax now. No one has ever fallen off this sleigh that I know of," he said Santa, chuckling.

"Santa, this ride is very smooth, it's just that this doesn't make a lot of sense to me."

"Explain yourself, what doesn't make a lot of sense?"

"We are very high off the ground, moving at an incredible speed and the temperature outside has to be below zero. The wind should be coming through here at over 100 miles an hour. We should be freezing."

"You've probably heard this a couple of times, 'It can't be explained in normal situations', it's called Christmas Magic," said Santa.

"Yes, I heard that many times," answered David.

Soon they arrived at the first house, landing on the roof. David remembered the part of the story where Santa and Sarah grew smaller in size. He examined the roof and chimney and decided that they too were miniaturized. "I see that we're smaller," said David.

"Yes, you'll get used to it quickly," said Santa.

Santa reached back into the sleigh and pulled out a sack of glowing gifts. "Come along, I'll show you how to use the chimney to get inside." Santa took a step and a hop and landed on the edge of the chimney. David took a step and a hop and he also landed on the edge of the chimney.

"Wow, that was so easy, I wish I could do that all the time," said David.

"Yes," said Santa. "Mrs. C enjoys this portion of the trip. We both wish we could do that every day, but it only works on Christmas."

"I'm going to put my finger on the side of my nose and gently stroke in a downward motion. If you do the same, you'll follow me into the house," said Santa.

Just like that, Santa disappeared. David thought to himself, "I've heard of a leap of faith, but this is the first time I will really leap."

David placed his finger on the side of his nose, closed his eyes and brushed downward. The next thing he knew, he was standing inside the house standing on the hearth of a fireplace. He was now larger in size but not his normal size. Santa was placing some of the gifts under the Christmas tree and other gifts into the stockings that were hung by the fireplace. "Come David, we have to be off, we have a lot of Christmas presents to deliver."

Quickly they were back on the hearth, Santa placed a finger on the side of his nose, took one step forward, brushed his nose, and disappeared. David followed the same procedure and found himself standing on the edge of the chimney. One hop, one step, and one rubbed nose, and he was back in the sleigh.

Santa shook the reins. The reindeer took three quick strides and were off one roof and almost instantly on another. In less than a blink of an eye, they delivered their packages and were off to another house. David was amazed how quickly and efficiently Santa was delivering the packages. "Santa, I get a feeling we're moving much faster than normal," said David.

"Yes, David, you are correct. We are moving so quickly that if those people were awake and could see us, we would just appear as a blur, a flash," he said.

Everything was routine until they reached a house where the lights were shining brightly. This time when they arrived at the hearth, the room appeared to be gigantic. David realized that both he and Santa were small, very small.

David looked into the living room and saw what appeared to be a mom, a dad, and two young children. They all appeared to be wide awake. David tapped Santa on his shoulder and whispered, "I think they're all awake."

Santa replied, "Yes, they are, but we are so tiny and moving at speeds they cannot comprehend, so they don't know we are here."

"Yes, but they'll see the gifts and know that we are here," said David.

"The gifts will remain tiny until they fall asleep. Then the gifts will regain their normal size."

David looked up at the people and saw that they were frozen in time. A small boy, probably five years old, was suspended in mid air. "He must've jumped on the couch and was falling at a very slow rate. This is where Einstein must've developed his idea that everything is relative," whispered David.

"I think you're probably correct. He was amazed when he observed something very similar to what you just saw."

They visited many, many houses, then they came upon one where the reindeer landed on the lawn rather than the roof. "Why are we landing here?" asked David.

"This house has no chimney. We'll still get inside, but will have to do it a little differently."

Santa took his sack that was filled with gifts that were glowing and said, "Follow me." He walked to the front door, laid his finger aside of his nose and disappeared. David wondered where Santa went, but reasoned if he did what Santa did, it should work. So David placed his finger aside of his nose and with a quick brush, instantly found himself inside the house.

"That was interesting, how we get in?" asked David.

"To be honest with you, I'm not sure, but it works. I've wondered about this for a long time. I think we sneak through any tiny crack. But I'm not sure," said Santa.

David was still in awe at how quickly everything was happening. And yet time seemed to be normal for him and Santa. They had time to talk, David asking questions and Santa answering them. As they landed on the roof of one house, David noticed there were palm trees. "Santa, how can we land on a roof that has no snow?"

"Well, you know about Snow's Flakes. The runners of this sleigh are coated with the flakes that Snow created from all the babies who were born since last Christmas. They are magical and they help us to land on snowless roofs."

"You can see that the number of presents that are left in the sleigh is dwindling down," said Santa. "So, we'll be heading back for more presents for the next part of our trip."

"Thank you Santa, it's been an amazing ride. I know this will go by quickly, but I do have a few more questions."

"Certainly, what are they?"

"How do you keep track of all the children and their requests?"

"There are a lot of children out there, but we have some help. Everyone has grandparents and great grandparents. When these people leave us, their spirits help us keep track of the children. We share a book with them, it's called the Big Book. They keep track of their children, grandchildren, and great grandchildren and make entries in the book. We use the Big Book to check on the children and their behaviors. Naturally, we are interested in those who have been naughty or nice."

"Do you see them? Can you see them?" asked David.

"No, we've never seen them, but when we open the book, the information is there."

"I never realized my grandparents and great grandparents still have an effect on my life. I guess they're still around," said David.

"Oh yes, they're still around and you know, they have visited you many times."

"Visited me, when?"

"Have you ever had snowflakes land on your eyelids?" asked Santa.

"Yes, it happened a few days ago when I was out on the ice."

"Those weren't just ordinary snowflakes, those were Snow's Flakes. She made the crystals of your grandparents and great grandparents when they were born. They just dropped by to say hello."

"Those snowflakes were my grandparents or great grandparents? They're still keeping watch over me?" asked David.

"Yes, David, your parents, your grandparents, and your great grandparents all watch out for you because they love you."

"Thank you for sharing that Santa," said David, tears welling up in his eyes. "That's wonderful. People should know about this."

"Now that you know that, maybe you should be pass that along so other people would know," said Santa.

"I'll have to think about that. I think I have some ideas," said David.

"I have another question. Do you ever make mistakes on who receives which presents?"

"Rarely, but it does happen. Children don't always get what they've asked for. For example, a child may asked for too many things. This is an example of a child being a child. Children need to learn that in their lives, there will be disappointments."

"Parents should not give their children everything, but make them earn it. They will have more respect for the things they earn than those things that are just given to them. When they're old enough, assign them chores to do around the house. Give them responsibilities. These assignments will help them develop self-discipline. Parents can assist their development by giving them surprise rewards. These rewards could be things like extra allowance, giving them the day off, or allowing them to stay up later. But don't make it routine, it has to be a surprise."

"In other words, don't spoil them. Also, children have to learn that when you misbehave, there are consequences."

"If a child doesn't respect themselves, other people, or other people's property, that child will have a difficult life. Parenting is not easy but is the most important part of a child's life. It's very difficult for a child to overcome bad parenting."

"Santa, I have one more question. I hope you won't think I'm too nosy but is Meghan an angel?"

"A very interesting question, and yes indeed, she is an angel."

"But she is so very young! Will she grow up into an adult?"

"She will remain as she is."

"Well, she's the first angel I ever met."

"No, David, you've met many angels, some very recently."

"Really? How would I know?"

"Think back. Can you remember a time when you were very, very lucky?"

"Well, not really."

"Do you remember the important meeting that you had in Boston when you left your wallet on a subway car?"

"Yes, it had all my money and it. I didn't even have a dime to make a phone call. I was unaware it slipped out of my pocket. As I left the subway car, something wasn't right. I reached back to check on my wallet as I usually do. It was gone! The doors closed before I could get back into the car. A young man called me and said, 'Hey mister, you left this on the train.' He handed my wallet back me and I tried to give him a $20 bill. He refused it. He didn't look like an angel. Thank God, he saved me. I would've missed the meeting and that would've been a disaster."

"Very few people realize when they are in contact with an angel," said Santa.

"Angels come in all shapes and sizes. Meghan is one who was sent by God to a family so she could learn what it would be like to be a human. They only stay with a family for a short period of time. It is heartbreaking for the moms, dads, brothers, and sisters the young angels leave behind. These families know that they have had an angel for a short time but they are grateful for the experience."

David remained quiet for a few minutes as he absorbed the conversation they just had. The thought ran through his mind, "Were Santa and Mrs. C both angels?" He decided not to ask that question. Some things are better off if they remain a mystery.

The sleigh was almost empty of Christmas gifts. David knew his once-in-a-lifetime trip was coming to an end. He looked out at the horizon where a faint hint of dawn could be seen. "I'm a lucky man," said David to himself.

Flying through the air in darkness is difficult to determine where you are in relation to the earth below. This is especially true if you're flying with Santa, his reindeer, and his sleigh. David had no clue where he was. The ground below was flying by and there was no way he could determine he was over his own hometown. The very first stop was at his own house, but he didn't even realize it. As usual, Santa and David took one step and one hop and they were standing on the edge of the chimney, ready to enter the house.

"David, why don't you go in first this time? I think you know how."

"Sure, just put my finger on the side of my nose. Give a gentle, stroke and..."

"Mommy, daddy, Santa's been here," said Kathy.

"Can we go downstairs now?" asked Jo, the quiet one, Kathy's younger sister.

David's two young daughters were draped over him and his wife Liz. He opened his eyes and realized he was in his own bed in his own house. He embraced the two young girls and his lovely life with more emotions that he felt in a long time.

"I didn't hear you come in last night," whispered Liz. "I'm surprised to find you here this morning," she said. "I know you can't talk about the mission, but it must've gone pretty smoothly."

David thought about what Liz just said. He wondered if the mission was real. Or was it all a dream?

"Mommy, daddy," said Kathy, while pulling on her parents' hands, "let's go see what Santa brought us."

"Please, please can we go downstairs now?" asked Jo.

Liz got up out of bed, put on her bathrobe and said, "Girls, daddy was up very late last night, making sure that Santa could get into the house okay, so we will go down in a minute."

"Daddy can go right now, he's okay," said David. "Let me put my on bathrobe and I'll be right behind you."

The two young daughters scrambled down the stairs, followed by their sleepy–eyed parents.

On the way downstairs, David whispered to Liz, "I had the most unbelievable realistic dream I've ever had."

"You'll have to tell me about it later," said Liz.

"See, see Santa was here," said Jo.

The girls knew there was an order that was always expected Christmas day. The rule was the youngest, Jo, would open one of her presents first, while the rest of the family would watch. Then Kathy would open one of her gifts. The two young children would alternate opening their gifts until all of their gifts would be opened. Then the two parents would open their gifts.

As Kathy was opening a gift, Liz, her brow wrinkled, said quietly to David, "That wrapping paper is new to me. That must be one you snuck in last night."

"No, you must be confused, I didn't bring that gift," said David.

"Oh sure, Santa dropped it off," said Liz sarcastically.

As Kathy tore the paper off and opened the package, David was stunned. "That looks like the sweater, *Mrs. C. was knitting while I was reading The Book,"* thought David.

Jo quickly opened the present with the same wrapping paper Kathy had. It was another sweater, just like the one Mrs. C had made.

David couldn't wait, he stood up, walked over to the Christmas tree, and picked up the two other packages with the same type of wrapping paper.

"Mommy and daddy are going to open up their presents now too," said David.

Liz gave David a look that was saying, "Why are you doing this?"

"Let's just open these gifts, I'm sure the girls will understand."

Liz opened up her package first and said, "This is beautiful, it's so well made and there's no tag on them. These are homemade. Where did you get them?"

"Well I met with Mrs. Santa Claus about making some sweaters for my family. And she promised me that you would love them. And I had Santa Claus deliver them late last night."

Liz gave David a hug and a kiss and said, "Tell Mrs. Claus that they are beautiful."

David sat down and pulled his pant leg up and looked at his left ankle. It was wrapped in an elastic bandage. David smiled as his family resumed opening their Christmas gifts.

Later that evening, Liz asked David where he purchased those sweaters.

He answered, "Well, I did go on a mission, I did meet some people, one of whom was a lady. A very nice lady who did some knitting. She was kind enough to make the sweaters. And I'm afraid I cannot tell you more than that."

218

Liz answered, "Yes, I know you can't tell me anything about the mission. I can live with that. But I do want to know one thing. Will there ever be a time when you could tell me something about what you have been doing?"

David took Liz into his arms and said, "Someday maybe I'll write a book."

About the Author

Ron Krzyzan was raised near the small upstate village of Marilla, New York. With no playmates his age, he created games and activities for himself. It was there that he developed his imagination. He was an active high school athlete, playing four sports. He liked school, but he loved sports.

His parents, grew up during the depression. Because of the economic times, both his father and mother had to find work to help their family's finances. Neither of them made it past the eighth grade.

With no role models, he did not consider education beyond high school. Upon graduation, he took on various jobs. Working in a supermarket, building toys at Fisher-Price and working on the New York Central Railroad.

While the railroad job gave him income, his love of sports caused him to rethink his future. His high school football coach helped him enter the University of Buffalo on a partial scholarship. He started on the freshman football team. He loved playing football but realized he was undersized to play that position on the varsity level. That, plus all of his teammates were living on campus while he was commuting to school. He felt like an outsider and decided to change schools where he could afford to live on campus.
He transferred to Brockport State University, a small upstate New York college. He had an interest in

science and took many electives in those subjects. He graduated with a degree in health and physical education.

His roommate Al, was a member of the cast of the school's production of the musical comedy Guys and Dolls. One spring day, Al announced that the cast of the play was invited by the USO to travel to Europe to entertain the troops. The next fall, they would travel through Germany and France for two months, performing at various Army and Air Force bases.

There was an opening in the play, Al told Ron to audition. Ron replied, "I can't act, I can't dance, I can't sing." Needless to say, Ron auditioned and won the part of Nathan Detroit.

The cast spent two months performing at Army and Air Force bases in Germany and France.

The year was 1961. Berlin was designated as a free and open city. It was also located deep in communist East Germany. The conditions In West Germany and West Berlin, were first rate. West Berlin was a vibrant and exciting city.

It was just the opposite in East Berlin. Life was difficult, material things food, clothing and other essentials were limited. Much of the population was unhappy, dissension was not tolerated. Many East Berliners defected to the West, and many died trying. To prevent East German citizens from escaping to West Berlin, the Berlin wall was constructed in

August. The wall completely surrounded West Berlin. The Cold War was on.

There were to be three performances in West Berlin. The group boarded a train in Frankfurt and traveled to the border of East Germany. They were crossing the Iron Curtain, and were only allowed to travel at night. Apparently the East German government did not want the group to see what the conditions were like.

It was dawn when the group arrived at once again crossed the Iron Curtain through the Berlin wall. The group's liaison officer, a young lieutenant asked the group if they would like to visit communist East Berlin. The vote was unanimous and they boarded a bus at about 9AM.

What occurred that day could have started World War III. The lieutenant gave instructions about taking photographs in East Berlin. "Don't take out your camera unless they tell you to. If you do, they may want to take your film, or your camera, or may want to arrest you." Obviously, no one took their cameras out.

They entered East Berlin through Checkpoint Charlie. This was the only exit and entry through the Berlin Wall for automobile traffic. As they crossed into East Berlin, the roadway was partially blocked by concrete barriers. These barriers were there to prevent East Berliners to escape by automobile. An automobile would have to slowly zigzag to get through the barriers. If an East Berliner tried this method of escape they surely would have been killed.

The bus had a much more difficult time but eventually passed through the barrier. They traveled to about 300 yards past Checkpoint Charlie, when it was stopped by an East German policemen. The liaison officer got off the bus and argued with the policeman.

The East German policeman wanted to see the groups' passports. Berlin was at that time, was an open city, no passports were required. The bus soon became surrounded by about 15 East German police officers. Each of them wore helmets and pointed machine guns at the bus.

Then things changed very quickly. The United States military went on full alert.

Ten US tanks pulled up to the wall. The tanks were equipped with bulldozer plows, designed to knock down the wall, if necessary. US jets were scrambled and patrolled overhead.

The lieutenant told a group that they were to wait for one hour for a Soviet officer to settle the dispute. The bus sat there for one hour, no Soviet officer appeared. The lieutenant instructed the bus driver to start the engine and to proceed. Three East German policemen stood in front of the bus pointing their guns at the driver.

Tension was very high when two American jeeps with MPs aboard drove to the front of the bus, almost running over the three East Germans. President Kennedy was awakened at 3:30 AM and was apprised of the situation. He ordered the bus to turn around and head back for West Berlin. It was a very short, interesting, exciting and scary tour of East Berlin.

Within a few hours Soviet tanks pulled up to within 100 yards of the US tanks. US soldiers and Soviet soldiers faced each other in full battle gear. The standoff lasted three days.

Ron has said, tongue-in-cheek, "Kennedy wanted to make sure that I was safe." They didn't perform the play that night, as all the soldiers were on full alert. They eventually did two shows.

The final five days of the trip was spent in Paris, and then back to the United States.

During that spring, Ron took advantage of the extra semester to take extra science classes. He already made the decision that he would become a science teacher.

His first teaching position was in the small village of Mount Morris, New York. His first year, he taught two seventh grade science classes, one senior health class and two physical education classes. The following year he became the junior high science teacher. He taught all the seventh and eighth grade classes.

A few years later, he took a teaching position at Gates Chili Central School, a suburb of Rochester, New York. Here he taught junior high science, as well as high school biology. He eventually retired after 32 years of service. During those years, he coached football, wrestling and basketball.

He is grateful to have a beautiful wife, three lovely daughters and seven wonderful grandchildren.